RESCUED BY A RANCHER

Mindy Neff

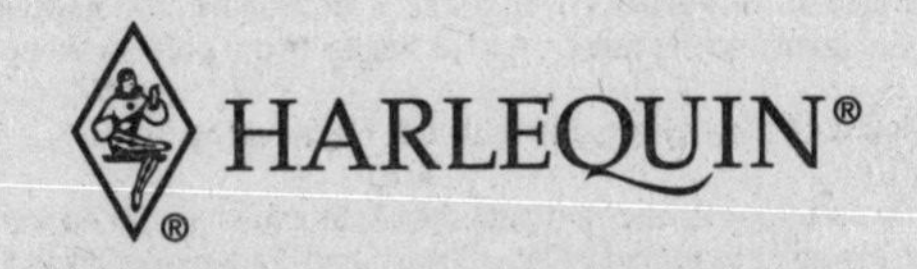

TORONTO • NEW YORK • LONDON
AMSTERDAM • PARIS • SYDNEY • HAMBURG
STOCKHOLM • ATHENS • TOKYO • MILAN • MADRID
PRAGUE • WARSAW • BUDAPEST • AUCKLAND

ISBN 0-373-75005-6

RESCUED BY A RANCHER

This edition published by arrangement with Harlequin Books S.A.

Visit us at www.eHarlequin.com

Printed in U.S.A.

ABOUT THE AUTHOR

Originally from Louisiana, Mindy Neff settled in Southern California, where she married a really romantic guy and raised five kids. Family, friends, writing and reading are her passions. When she's not writing, Mindy's ideal getaway is a good book, hot sunshine and a chair at the river's edge with water lapping at her toes.

Books by Mindy Neff

HARLEQUIN AMERICAN ROMANCE

809—A PREGNANCY AND A PROPOSAL
830—THE RANCHER'S MAIL-ORDER BRIDE
834—THE PLAYBOY'S OWN MILLIONAIRE
838—THE HORSEMAN'S CONVENIENT WIFE
857—THE SECRETARY GETS HER MAN
898—CHEYENNE'S LADY
906—PREACHER'S-IN-NAME-ONLY WIFE
925—IN THE ENEMY'S EMBRACE
946—THE INCONVENIENTLY ENGAGED PRINCE

Chapter One

Sometimes a woman had to take charge of her own destiny. Tracy Lynn Randolph was doing just that.

Above her, puffy clouds cast huge shadows over the Texas hills, the sky so blue it almost hurt to look at it. A brisk November wind ruffled the spiky seed pods on the sweet-gum tree, scattering little sticker balls over the lawn and onto the steps of the redbrick courthouse.

Even if it hadn't been such a glorious afternoon, nothing could have dampened Tracy Lynn's mood. Her smile far outshone any smile she'd perfected in the dozen or so beauty pageants she'd entered in her youth. She pressed a hand to her chest as if to contain her giddy excitement.

Pausing at the base of the Hope Valley courthouse steps, she closed her eyes and sent her thoughts heavenward.

Mama, are you watching? I'm finally starting on my dream. Our dream.

Her heart squeezed and her throat ached as she remembered the words her mother had uttered just hours before succumbing completely to the aggressive ovarian cancer that had been draining the life from her once-vibrant body for the past eight months.

"Give Daddy grandbabies," Mama had said, her voice weak yet steady. "You were the only child I was able to have, and he so wanted a big family."

"I will, Mama. Before I'm thirty."

In those last few weeks they'd planned Tracy Lynn's future—a future her mother, Chelsa, would never see, the fairy-tale wedding she would never attend. They'd even chosen names for the grandbabies, whose sweet, warm bodies her mother would never rock in her arms.

Those had been the very best weeks of Tracy Lynn's life. And the very worst.

Ten years had gone by since her mom had died. Tracy Lynn had truly believed she'd be married long before she turned twenty-five—a reasonable assumption since she'd *never* lacked for dates.

But Prince Charming hadn't arrived.

So she'd decided to go on without him.

Granted, she hadn't actually met the deadline she'd so confidently promised her mother, but she was darn close. Next month, on Christmas Eve, she'd be turning thirty.

Before that auspicious day, though, she would be able to tell her dad that he was going to be a grandpa. The thought of Hope Valley Mayor Jerald Randolph bouncing his grandbaby on his knee was enough to make Tracy Lynn laugh out loud.

She looked up as her dad pushed through the glass

doors of the courthouse. He was a handsome man at fifty-nine, his dark hair graying at the temples, giving him a distinguished look. He was also still quite slim, due in part to his restless energy.

Jerald Randolph didn't know how to relax; he had to be going somewhere or doing something all the time.

She waved and jogged up the half-dozen steps to meet him on the wide landing and give him a hug. "Hey, Daddy."

His frown was both apologetic and confused as he pecked her on the cheek. "Did I forget an appointment, honey?"

"No. But I have some great news, and I couldn't wait to share it."

"Can you tell me in three minutes or less? You caught me on the way to a meeting."

"I know. I called Alice and she itemized your schedule." His secretary knew more about him than anyone else. Tracy Lynn had hoped to get her father alone so they could celebrate in private, but the man was a workaholic—had been all her life—and she'd learned to catch him when she could, often obliged to fall into step beside him as he rushed from one place to the next, conducting his mayoral duties or handling his commercial-real-estate-investment business.

"That's why I wanted to intercept you this afternoon, so you'd be the first to know. It's all I can do not to climb the flagpole and shout it to the world."

He gave her an indulgent smile. "In the interest

of decorum, why don't you just tell me and I'll pass along whatever it is at the school-board meeting. That'd be a lot more effective. Those folks can spread news faster than a minnow can swim a dipper.''

Although he was smiling at her, she noticed that he looked pale, tired. But her fabulous announcement would perk him up for sure.

She took a breath, felt her eyes mist from happiness.

''You're going to be a grandfather, Dad.''

He looked at her in confusion.

''I'm pregnant.''

Dead silence met her words. Instead of the awe and exuberant hug she'd expected, his smile faded and his facial muscles went rigid.

A sparrow hopped off a nearby brick planter, then darted away in a flutter of wings. Somewhere, a woodpecker hammered his beak into bark in search of supper, the staccato sound matching the rhythm of Tracy Lynn's heart.

Dread began to gather beneath her sternum as she waited for him to respond. Although they were the only two standing on the steps, he glanced around as if checking to see if anyone might have overheard her announcement.

This wasn't the proud reception she'd expected. He appeared…embarrassed.

''Daddy?'' she prompted. ''Aren't you excited?''

Gripping her upper arm, he pulled her to one side

of the landing, next to the iron bench and metal ash can county employees used during smoke breaks.

"What do you mean, you're pregnant?" The question was a harsh demand. His gaze darted to her stomach, then back to her face. "Did you think this was good news? You're not even married, Tracy Lynn."

"Oh, Daddy." She smiled and shook her head. "That's not an issue in this generation."

"You damned well better believe it is in *my* generation! It's vitally important for our family to keep up a good image. If I run for senator, you can be sure my opponent will dig deep in our backyard, searching for old bones we can't bury. My God, girl, you know how gossip is in a small town."

"But this is *good* gossip. There's no need to hide my pregnancy or the existence of my child." The sting of rejection swarmed in her stomach like angry bees. She was both bewildered and terrified.

For the first time in her life, she wasn't Daddy's perfect girl. And she didn't know quite how to react.

Jerald reached for his handkerchief and mopped his brow. "Who's the father?"

"No one..." The gray pallor of his skin worried her, cutting off her explanation. He was breathing heavily, and she'd never seen him sweat so profusely. "Daddy? What's wrong?"

"Nothing. I asked you a question, girl. I—" He opened his mouth to continue, but his face contorted in pain. To her everlasting horror, he clutched his chest, and before her brain could signal her to reach out and catch him, he collapsed at her feet, his back scraping against the iron bench as he went down.

"Oh, my God! Daddy! Somebody, help!" She wasn't sure if she managed to yell loud enough for anyone inside the courthouse to hear. Her purse slid off her shoulder as she dropped to her knees beside him.

She couldn't think, couldn't breathe. She felt as though she was having a nightmare—this couldn't be happening! Every bit of first-aid training she'd ever learned—she'd needed it to care for her mother and later to work at the senior center—flew right out of her head.

"Don't do this to me, girl." He wheezed and gasped for breath. "I can't have my daughter pregnant and not married. Tell me. We'll make everything right. I need to know who fathered this baby—"

"I did, sir."

Tracy Lynn turned quickly to see who had spoken. Lincoln Slade—bad-boy-turned-rancher. She watched, heart in her throat, as Linc bent down, loosened Jerald's shirt buttons, looked him straight in the eye and said, "Now, let's calm down and leave this discussion until later."

Tracy Lynn was so distraught she could hardly think past the fact that her strong, youthful father was lying at the top of the courthouse steps gasping for breath. In some rational part of her mind, she noted that Linc already had his cell phone against his ear.

Oh, God. Hers was in her purse. She hadn't even thought—

"I need rescue in front of the courthouse," Linc said into the phone. "Patients name is Jerald Randolph. Early sixties. Appears to be a heart attack. Tell the paramedics that if they look out their door, they'll see us."

"Do you have any aspirin, babe?"

"I have Tylenol." She snatched up her purse, dumping the contents on the cement. "Will that work? Wait. Maybe I've got—"

Linc swore.

Her head jerked up, fear ripping at her insides.

Her father's eyes had rolled back in his head.

His chest wasn't moving.

Linc dropped the phone and went into action.

Paralyzed by shock, Tracy Lynn stared as he checked her father's pulse, his breathing, then shook him and shouted his name. Only seconds passed before he tilted back her daddy's head, breathed deeply into his mouth, then began CPR compressions.

"Breathe for him, Trace," Linc said. "I'll pause on ten. Come on, now. Get it together."

Her hands were shaking so hard she could barely position her father's chin.

"And nine, and ten," Linc counted. "Now!"

Tears streaming down her cheeks, she tried to blow air into her father's mouth, but terror and anguish made her own breath shallow. She choked on a sob, didn't even have enough air in her lungs to lift his chest.

"Damn it, Tracy Lynn. Snap out of it!" Linc resumed chest compressions, palms cupped, counting even as he shouted at her. "This isn't about you, Princess. Now breathe for him or kiss him goodbye!"

Tears dripping onto her father's face, she did as she was told, Linc's forceful words finally penetrating her stupor. Between Linc's compressions, she transferred her breath into her father's lungs for what seemed like hours.

At last sirens screamed from half a block away. Tracy Lynn wondered why in heaven's name the paramedics hadn't just grabbed their gear and run the short distance.

As she bent to cover his mouth once more, Jerald took a breath. His eyes opened and he looked around wildly as though he had no idea how he'd ended up lying on the cold concrete.

Paramedics appeared at her elbow. One of them was Damian Stoltz. She'd dated him a couple of years ago, but things hadn't worked out between them.

She felt Linc's hands on her, urging her to her feet, shifting her out of the way so the medics would have room to work. Her body trembled and her teeth chattered, more from fear than the chilly afternoon air.

"You did just fine, babe," Linc said, drawing her against his side, his hands chafing her arms, her back, bringing warmth to thaw the icy shock.

She shook her head, didn't deserve his bolstering. She'd been worse than useless, frozen in blind terror when she should have acted. "He wasn't breathing. His heart stopped. Linc, what if—"

"Shh. He's in good hands now."

The other paramedic was Mason Lowe, whom she'd also dated. Thank heaven she remained friends with guys when the relationships didn't work. She'd never seen Damian or Mason so serious and efficient.

Or Linc, either.

She leaned into his warmth. He'd only been back in Hope Valley for four months, showing up the day his brother, Jackson Slade, had married Sunny Carmichael—who happened to be the town's veterinarian and one of Tracy Lynn's best friends.

"I'm so glad you were here," she said.

He didn't respond. Lincoln Slade was one of those men who could be stingy with words.

Just when she thought her nerves were about to get a reprieve, there was a scurry of activity and a volley of words between Damian and Mason.

"V-fib," Damian said. "Charging to two-hundred joules."

Daddy! Tracy Lynn automatically lunged forward, but Linc hooked his arm around her waist and held her back.

"What's wrong? What are they doing?" She could hear the fear in her voice as she struggled against Linc's hold. "Let me go. I need to see what's happening."

"Shh." He pressed his mouth to her hair near her ear. "Let the professionals do their work, babe."

Her fingernails dug into the sleeve of his brown

suede jacket, his arm remaining as taut as a safety harness around her middle. One of the monitors on the ground emitted an escalating whine. A discarded wrapper, ripped open in haste, skipped away with the wind, tumbling across the courthouse lawn.

"Everybody stay back," Mason said, quickly checking to ensure their compliance. "I'm clear," he said. "You're clear. Everybody's clear. Shocking at two hundred joules."

Tracy Lynn realized what was going on a bare instant before the defibrillator paddles sent an audible jolt through her father's body, a jolt that lifted his upper body right off the ground.

"Nothing!" Mason reported. "Charging again to three hundred."

She couldn't watch. Twisting in Linc's arms, she rested her forehead against his chest and gripped the lapels of his sheepskin-lined suede jacket, horribly aware of her own moan as the second shock, then a third reverberated behind her.

Linc's hand cupped the back of her head, applying firm and steady pressure, his other hand stroking the length of her back over her cashmere sweater. His hold was both comforting and protective, shielding her whether she wanted him to or not.

If she'd been capable of speech, she would have told him that there was no danger of her stealing a look.

She couldn't bear to watch another parent die before her eyes.

"They've got him back," he whispered against her hair, loosening his hold.

Her fingers relaxed their grip on the lapels of his jacket. She filled her lungs with the chill air and stepped back. "Thanks for the shoulder—or the chest, rather." She smiled weakly.

"Anytime."

"We'll transport your father to Mercy General," Damian said as Mason finished inserting the IV he'd had to abandon moments ago.

Hope Valley was a small blip on the map west of Austin. Although they had a fully staffed medical clinic here in town, Mercy General, which was a little farther away, was better equipped to handle a cardiac patient.

"May I ride with him?" She was dry-eyed now. Her body and mind were simply too numb for tears.

"Of course," Mason answered, his eyes kind as he stood. "We've got room."

As they strapped Jerald onto a gurney, she thought briefly about the subject that had apparently brought on Daddy's heart attack. It was clear he wanted the news of her baby kept under wraps. He ought to consider a future behind a pulpit, rather than a seat in the senate. He was darn good at making an innocent person feel like a sinner.

Nausea welled as she watched the medics wheel him to the ambulance. She took several deep breaths against the memories pelting her, the memories of all the times she'd ridden in the back of medical vehicles with her mother when the cancer had gotten bad.

Daddy had never been with them, she realized now. She'd always had to call him at work and let him know to meet them at the hospital. Odd that she'd never thought of this before, how little he'd been around during those final days. In the end, Tracy Lynn's arms were the ones holding her mother, easing her passage into death.

Linc squeezed her shoulder. "I'll follow you in my truck."

For a moment, she'd forgotten he was there, which was pretty amazing. Lincoln Slade wasn't the kind of man a person easily forgot. His six-foot-four frame alone commanded attention.

"You don't have to drive all the way out to Mercy," she said,

He smoothed his hand along her hair. "You'll need a ride home, babe."

"I can get a cab."

"That'd be silly since I'm offering." He urged her toward the ambulance. "I'll meet you there."

LINC WATCHED HER CLIMB into the back of the ambulance. A few employees from the courthouse had gathered outside the glass doors, keeping a respectful distance. Linc barely glanced in their direction.

He went down the courthouse steps and climbed into his truck, then fell in behind the ambulance as it traveled down Main Street and turned onto the two-lane highway heading east toward Austin. His mind kept flipping back to the astonishing fact that Tracy Lynn was pregnant.

Man alive, he hadn't expected that. And he hadn't been prepared for the jealousy he was feeling now, jealousy regarding the real father of her child.

Despite his quick actions, his nerves weren't all that steady. He'd never imagined he'd find himself in the position of saving Jerald Randolph's life, and he didn't mind admitting that the whole episode shook him up.

Now that he mentally replayed the scene, he felt bad about hollering at Tracy Lynn. Man, the anguish in those blue eyes had nearly flayed him alive.

He'd always been a little in love with her, but any fool knew that the socialite and the son of the town drunk weren't a good combination. Her daddy had made that quite clear when Linc had walked her home from school one day years ago after a group of bullies had cornered her and scared the bejeebers out of her.

A lot had changed since then, though. Anger, dogged determination and a knack with horses made him one of the top Thoroughbred breeders in the state of Texas. Hell, he could buy this town—including Jerald Randolph—and still have money in the bank.

Not that he still bore Randolph a grudge. Truthfully, he didn't give a damn about anyone's opinion of him. Most of his life he'd been labeled a bad boy, the kid from the wrong side of the tracks, and sometimes he deliberately made it a point to maintain that reputation.

It remained to be seen if the good mayor still judged a man by where he came from, or if he recognized and appreciated the changes a man could make in his life. When they'd worked side by side updating Donetta Presley-Carmichael's hair salon a few weeks back, Jerald hadn't reacted to him one way or the other.

But the man had sure blown a gasket today.

Blue-and-red flashing lights chased across the bar on top of the paramedic van, the vivid strobes clearly visible even in the bright afternoon sun. He could see Tracy Lynn's blond hair through the back windows.

Hearts would be breaking all over town when news got out that Tracy Lynn Randolph was pregnant.

Like her father, Linc wanted to know who the daddy was. There had to be a story, otherwise she'd have come clean right off when Jerald asked her for a name.

He sure hadn't anticipated being trapped into eavesdropping on Tracy Lynn's conversation with her father when he'd pushed through the courthouse door and stepped outside. They'd been off to the side of the door by the wrought-iron bench, but they might as well have been square in the middle of his path.

His gut had twisted when he'd realized Jerald was berating her right there in public. Never mind that he'd been the only one around to witness it.

All he'd been able to think about were the memories of his own father shouting, swinging his arm with an open palm aimed at his head. Or a bullwhip lashing the tender skin on his back.

The best decision Linc had made back then was to hightail his backside out of Hope Valley at the first opportunity—which happened to fall at the wise old age of seventeen. Ever since, he couldn't abide bullies or seeing anyone being taken advantage of.

He was a champion for the underdog, and in that one moment this afternoon, Tracy Lynn had appeared in need of rescue.

Then Jerald had collapsed, and Linc's only thought had been to get the situation under control. Telling the mayor that he'd gotten his daughter pregnant was a little extreme, but it had been a snap decision, the only way he'd seen at the time to bring about some calm.

No big deal, he told himself. They'd just explain later when Jerald wasn't in danger of having another heart attack.

As he followed the paramedics into the emergency parking lot entrance to the hospital, he picked up his cell phone. Tracy Lynn would want her friends to know what was going on.

The Texas Sweethearts, they called themselves.

The four women—Sunny Carmichael-Slade, Donetta Presley-Carmichael, Becca Sue Ellsworth and Tracy Lynn Randolph had all grown up together and were still a tight group, even though two had married—Sunny to his brother and Donetta to Sunny's brother, Sheriff Storm Carmichael. Linc didn't understand that kind of closeness, the genuine love and trust the four women felt for one another.

He mostly kept to himself. The solitary lifestyle worked for him, and he liked it just fine.

And he sure as hell wouldn't trust anyone with his heart.

Chapter Two

Linc parked his truck and went into the emergency room waiting area.

Within twenty minutes, he was surrounded by Sunny, Donetta and Becca, all of them bombarding him with questions. The speed with which they'd made it to the hospital was impressive.

All three were working women with busy afternoons—Sunny doctored the animals in town, Donetta did hairdos at her salon, and Becca Sue sold folks antiques, books and designer coffee at her shop. Clearly they'd dropped what they were doing and just raced out the door.

"I'm going back there to see what's happening," Sunny said in the no-nonsense tone she used when bossing around cows four times her size.

"I already tried," Donetta said, giving an indelicate snort. She still wore her black vinyl bib apron that had her salon's name, Donetta's Secret, emblazoned across the front. "The emergency room Gestapo with the hideous perm ran me off without an ounce of consideration for my delicate condition."

She cradled an abdomen that barely showed her pregnancy. ''The old bat wouldn't even tell Tracy Lynn I was here.''

Sunny put her hands on her hips, dislodging animal hairs clinging to her white lab coat. ''I'm a doctor. I can get in there.''

''You're a veterinarian,'' Becca Sue corrected. ''This is a people hospital, in case you haven't noticed. Your credentials won't mean squat here.''

''Gaining entrance to restricted areas is all in the attitude,'' Sunny said. ''You just have to act like you know what you're doing, like you belong. Besides, we can't just let Tracy Lynn sit back there by herself. Come on. We'll all four go. They can't stop the whole bunch of us, and if they try, Linc can run interference.''

''I don't think there'll be any need,'' Linc said, nodding in the direction of the emergency room doors.

They all turned as Tracy Lynn walked out. She looked lost, sad, flustered and seriously peeved. Quite a combination, he thought. He hoped the last emotion wasn't directed at him.

When she spotted them, it seemed as though she singled him out of the group. Something in his chest gave way when she met his gaze, her beautiful features sliding into relief as if he alone held up her world.

Hell, where did that sappy thought spring from?

She headed toward them, her boot heels clicking against the tiled floor.

"Linc called us," Donetta said, and with Sunny and Becca Sue pulled Tracy Lynn close.

Linc felt a peculiar pang of envy as he watched the four-way hug. He'd lived in this town from birth through high school, yet, other than his brother, Jack, he didn't have any special friends.

"How's your dad doing?" Sunny asked Tracy Lynn when at last the foursome pulled apart.

"He's awake and trying to tell the doctors how to do their jobs. They took him down to the radiology department. I suppose we'll know more once they do a few tests."

"How about you?" Linc asked. "You holding up okay?"

"If the billing people would quit hounding me about insurance forms, I'd be doing a lot better. Daddy's the mayor, for goodness' sake. It's not as though they wouldn't be able to find him if he skipped out on the bill. I tell you, these places just make me so mad. You'd think they'd have a little compassion for family members who are upset."

Linc patted her shoulder. She was working herself into a state. "Want me to go beat them up?"

She gaped at him in surprise. Then she laughed. A dimple winked at the corner of her mouth, and he took a step back, because he was way too tempted to press his lips just there.

"That's a tempting offer, but I'll pass, thanks. I'm sorry for leaving you all out here like this. Linc, you really didn't need to stay."

He tugged at the brim of his hat. "I promised you

a ride home. I try to make it a point to leave with the same lady I arrive with.''

''Nice trait.'' She tucked a strand of blond hair behind her ear. ''Do you also make it a point to claim responsibility for her pregnancy?''

''Can't say as I've had that come up before.'' He liked her moxie, especially when he could see the worry in her blue eyes.

After what appeared to be a synchronized, delayed reaction, Sunny, Becca Sue and Donetta gasped and started talking all at once.

''What?''

''I thought you were—''

''You guys got together? I—''

''Shh!'' Tracy Lynn hissed, conscious of the hospital personnel nearby. She looked at Linc.

''I didn't tell them about that part.'' He winked and sauntered off toward the chairs.

Tracy Lynn's yearning to have a child was something she'd shared with only her three closest friends. For a few moments, her initial giddy excitement flared as she repeated the news of her positive pregnancy test. Then it died when she told them how upset her father became and Linc's astonishingly generous, and ultimately fruitless effort to calm him.

''I thought Daddy would be thrilled. Instead, I gave him a heart attack. Literally.''

''Oh, you did not,'' Donetta said, then looked over at Sunny for confirmation. ''Did she?''

Becca nudged Donetta's shoulder. ''Real good,

Donetta. Has pregnancy fried your brain cells, or what?''

Donetta gave Becca a ''so bite me'' look.

''You didn't cause the heart attack, Tracy Lynn,'' Sunny said with soothing authority.

Donetta reached for Tracy Lynn's hand. ''I understand how your father might worry about whispering campaigns and the opinion of others. Remember how I acted when I found out I was pregnant? I was convinced the gossipmongers would have a field day with me, and that it would spill over onto Storm and his job as sheriff. But the Darla Pam Kirkwells of the world don't stand a chance against all of us.''

''I'm sure your dad was just caught off guard,'' Becca said. ''Once he's had a chance to think clearly, when he's not suffering with the pain of a heart attack, he'll be a proud, expectant grandpa.''

That remained to be seen. And, if he did indeed run for a seat on the senate, the repercussions Jerald Randolph worried about had the potential to reach national levels— way out of Darla Pam Kirkwell's range.

Meanwhile, Tracy Lynn really needed to talk to Linc. In private.

''I hope you're right. I've had my heart set on having a baby for so long, and I'd hate to think that the very thing I want most might cause dissension between Daddy and me. But right now, you all need to get back to work.''

''To hell with work,'' Sunny said. ''You're more important.''

"And I love you for that. But I'm okay. I don't know how long it'll be before they get Daddy settled in a room. There's no sense in all of us sitting around here waiting. I'll call if anything comes up, okay?"

"He's just as important to us," Becca reminded her. "You don't need to go through this alone."

"I'm not alone."

She glanced over at Linc. He was slouched in an upholstered chair, his coffee-brown hat pulled low on his brow as though he was trying to catch a little sleep. What was it about a man in a cowboy hat? she wondered. The mystique? He could cast a glance from beneath the brim, a glance that might spell invitation or censure, promise or threat. A frisson of excitement shivered up her spine to the roots of her hair.

She reined in her curiosity over Lincoln Slade's magnetism. "I need to speak with Linc. We'll have to get our stories straight about the baby—at least until Daddy is stable."

"I can't decide if I'm surprised by Linc's actions or not," Sunny said. "He's got a good heart, but he's a hard one to figure out. He's not normally the kind of guy to butt in." Since Sunny was married to Linc's brother, she probably knew him the best. But that wasn't saying much—Linc didn't allow people to get close.

"Well, at least he's cute and rich," Becca Sue commented. "Just think, if it had been Artie Bertram who'd come to your rescue, your daddy would be imagining a stick-skinny grandkid with axle grease under his nails.''

''And acne scars,'' Donetta added.

''Thank you for putting that picture in my mind,'' Tracy Lynn said dryly. ''Especially since my sperm donor was anonymous. Go back to work, would you? All of you.''

The women grinned and acquiesced. ''You'll call and keep us up-to-date on your dad's prognosis?'' Becca asked.

''You know I will.'' She hugged her girlfriends, feeling fortunate to have such tight friendships. She never thought of herself as an only child, because she'd always had Sunny, Donetta and Becca Sue as surrogate sisters.

The Texas Sweethearts, friends through thick and thin.

When the women left, promising to come back after work, Tracy Lynn crossed to Linc and sat down beside him.

''Did you run them off?'' he asked, his chin still tucked to his chest, his hat pulled low.

''Yes. And you really don't have to stay, either.''

He lifted his head. ''Why are you trying so hard to get rid of everyone?''

''I'm not. But there's nothing anyone can do at this point, so it's silly to sit out here in the waiting room.''

''If I wanted to do something...silly, I suppose that'd be my prerogative. Been a long time since I've done anything I didn't want to.''

"Really? If that's the case, what in heaven's name possessed you to tell my father that my baby is yours? Do you realize what you've done?"

"Babe, the man's heart was threatening to cash in his chips, and I sure didn't hear *you* coming forth with a name."

"That's because there isn't one!"

He folded his arms across his chest. Other than his gaze dipping to her flat stomach, his expression hardly changed. He merely waited for her to elaborate.

"I had artificial insemination about three weeks ago. You've heard of that, haven't you?"

"I'm aware of the term. A good portion of my breeding operation involves artificially inseminating the mares. Why didn't you just say so when your dad asked?"

"There wasn't time. I mean, I would have...I was just so excited, I blurted it out." She stood and began pacing. "I used one of those home-test kits, and when it came up positive, I rushed over to the courthouse."

"Couldn't wait till suppertime?"

"We're close, Daddy and me." She shoved her hair back from her forehead. "I never even considered the possibility that he wouldn't be pleased about the baby." She realized that she had a tendency to plow headlong into ventures, automatically expecting them to turn out fine. Sure, she'd gotten herself into some fixes over the years, but she was usually lucky and eventually things fell into place.

This time, she wasn't quite as confident. Her reputation wasn't the only one at stake. Her father's was, as well.

"He didn't know you were trying to get pregnant?"

"No. I couldn't see any sense in both of us getting our hopes up, watching the calendar and wringing our hands. You have no idea how stressful this is. And now...I still can't figure out what in the world you were thinking when you claimed paternity. You've gotten us into a bigger mess."

"Come on, babe. It's not as bad as you think." He stood and moved toward her. "We'll just leave things be for now and straighten out everything when your dad recovers."

"You mean, pretend I've been sleeping with you?"

His brows slammed down. "I imagine you could do worse. For the record, I bathe daily and I've had all my shots."

She sighed. "I didn't mean to sound like..." She waved her hand, the word escaping her.

"A society girl?"

Her head snapped up. "It used to make me very mad when you called me that."

"I know." He paused, letting the implication of the words sink in.

His direct stare made her heart skip. He was toying with her. Did he have any idea what that had done to her as a girl? What it did to her as a woman?

"What were you doing at the courthouse, anyway?'' she asked, trying to find the solid ground beneath her feet.

The corners of his mouth curled up. ''The building houses other departments besides the ones where you pay fines and go before the judge, babe.''

She opened her mouth, closed it, then frowned. ''That wasn't necessary, Lincoln Slade. I didn't automatically assume you were there because you were in trouble.''

He shrugged. ''I was looking up county records on some property boundaries. There's a seven-hundred-acre parcel I want to buy.''

''The way you and your brother have been acquiring land, I thought you already owned every plot of open range around here.''

''Not every plot...yet,'' he added with a half grin. ''Jack's been gnashing his teeth over a pie-shape wedge of land that's smack dab in the center of his north section. He bought up the parcels all around it and doesn't like giving easement rights—even though the owners live in New Jersey. I might have to make an offer above market value to get the title holders to turn loose, but the investment will pay for itself.''

''You've done really well for yourself since you left Hope Valley.''

He tugged at the brim of his hat. ''Horses are easy.''

''But land and people are hard?''

''People are. Most of the time.''

''What about me?'' she asked, having no idea

what propelled her. Frayed nerves, she decided. "Am I hard?"

He touched her cheek, his knuckle stroking lightly, his eyes steady on hers. "You're silky soft."

"That's not what I meant."

His lips curved in what could have passed for a smile if he'd put a little effort into it. "I like to see you blush. And it's not often a person gets a front-row seat to witness the cool Tracy Lynn Randolph in a state of panic."

"I did not panic." She'd done exactly that.

Replaying the drama in her mind filled her with embarrassment. She wanted to ask him if she'd caused this game of pretense they found themselves in. She'd never felt or acted so helpless in her life. Had she subconsciously wanted someone to rescue her? Had he seen that panic in her eyes and mistaken it for something else, something that caused him to step in and claim paternity?

She laid a hand on his forearm, surprised when he maneuvered so that her palm slid down his wrist and into *his* hand.

"Thank you for saving my father's life. After Mama...I don't think I could bear losing Daddy, too."

"He's young, Trace. And strong. Hell, I worked beside him at Donetta's beauty shop and he swung a hammer as easily as any of the rest of us."

"Typical. If work is involved, he'll be the last man to pack up and go home." She glanced toward the emergency room, wondered how long it would take for the X rays. "You know, you took a pretty big risk laying claim to my baby. The additional shock could have made Daddy worse."

"I may not have been good enough before, babe, but that's all changed." His tone was slightly defensive. "I've got a bank account that ensures no one closes a door on me."

She wondered how many doors had been slammed in his face before success and money had given him the clout and prestige he enjoyed today.

"I'm sorry," she said softly. "I keep saying the wrong thing. People treat me differently because of the size of my trust fund, and I've simply accepted it as part of life. But you've experienced both ends of the spectrum." Her father had called him a hoodlum when he was in high school. "You're right, though. Daddy is swayed by things like monetary success. But I'm not."

Amusement flashed in his eyes and she realized she'd blundered into insult again. "I meant that I've never judged you," she said.

He didn't comment. Silence stretched as he watched her, his gray-blue eyes giving away none of his emotions.

"Can I buy you a cup of coffee?" he asked.

He'd changed the subject in a way that left no room for negotiation. Tracy Lynn wasn't used to someone else having the upper hand in a conversation, but with Lincoln Slade she couldn't seem to find her usual pluck. This wasn't a man who'd fall at a woman's feet and let her call the shots, as so many of the men she'd dated had.

Was that her problem? That she hadn't yet met a man who challenged her?

"I don't want to leave the waiting area in case the doctor comes out."

"Okay. We can take our chances with the complimentary mud over there in the pot, or I can go scare us up a decent cup."

She wasn't a clinging kind of woman, but she didn't want to be alone, even for the short time it would take him to go to the hospital cafeteria and back. And that was ridiculous. For goodness' sake, she'd sent her friends home.

"I suppose we could live dangerously and give this stuff a try—" She stopped, her eyes growing wide. "What am I thinking? I'm pregnant. I shouldn't be drinking coffee in the first place."

His gaze moved to her stomach. For no accountable reason, chills raced up and down her spine. She didn't know the name of her sperm donor, which was the way she'd wanted it. She was, after all, a single mother by choice.

But she couldn't help wondering how it would feel to have the father of her child standing here beside her, sharing her worry, caressing her still-flat stomach with his eyes, imagining the life he'd helped to create growing within her womb.

And she couldn't stop herself from casting Lincoln Slade in that role.

"If we're not going to have coffee, let's sit." Linc

put his hand at her waist and led her over to the chairs. "So, what do you do?" he asked.

"Do?" She sat. "Like a job?"

"Most people have one."

"I guess I'm what you'd call a philanthropist. I have a trust fund that allows me to live comfortably on just the interest. So I try to give back to the community—mainly through charities involving senior citizens, children and the hospital. And after Mama died, I took over as hostess for Daddy. He does a lot of political entertaining. It keeps me busy."

"What made you decide to have a kid on your own? And what's the matter with the men in this town to let a thing like that happen?"

"There's nothing wrong with being a single mother," she defended. "As for the men in town, I think I intimidate them. I'll be thirty at the end of the year..."

"Christmas Eve," he murmured.

"How do you know my birthday?"

"Mine's Christmas Day. Your folks used to have a party for you every year at the country club. I worked there for a couple of years, helped get the banquet room ready." Actually, he'd fantasized that she was his birthday and Christmas gift rolled into one.

"Oh." She shifted uncomfortably, glanced away. "Anyway, I wanted a baby before I turned thirty, and since I don't have any husband prospects, I decided to take control. My first round didn't work. So

I had a second procedure—'' She stopped speaking when the emergency room doors swung open.

The cardiologist she'd met earlier scanned the waiting room.

Tracy Lynn jumped up and rushed forward to meet him. ''Dr. Bruley. How is he?''

''Well, considering he suffered an acute myocardial infarction, he's—''

''What's a myocardial infarction?''

''Heart attack.''

''But he's only fifty-nine!'' Then again, Mama had only been forty-eight when she'd died. The thought sneaked through Tracy Lynn's battered defenses.

''Heart disease isn't limited to the elderly.'' Although the doctor's demeanor suggested he was in a hurry, his eyes remained kind. ''How long has your father had high blood pressure?''

''He doesn't—I mean, no one's ever said so. *He* hasn't said so.''

''He should have been on meds and under the care of a cardiologist long before this,'' the doctor said.

''Did his blood pressure cause the heart attack?''

''It's possible. I can't say for sure until I run more tests. We'll be keeping him here for a while. The nurses are getting him settled in CCU.''

''But he was awake and talking in the emergency room. I thought he was going to be fine.''

Linc put his arm around her shoulders, the touch making her aware that her voice was rising in fear.

She took a breath, tried to stay calm. That was like

asking an elephant to squeeze through a mouse hole. Impossible.

"We've got him pumped full of morphine, and he's in cardiac arrhythmia, so—"

"Do you mind saying that in layman's terms?" Linc asked. Tracy Lynn gave him a grateful look.

"Sorry." The cardiologist shook his head. "His heart is beating erratically. We doctors prefer steady rhythm. Mr. Randolph has agreed to an angiogram, and I've scheduled it for tomorrow morning. That's a procedure where we insert dye into the coronary arteries to check for blockage. After that, we'll know better what we're dealing with."

"What if there's blockage?"

"Depending on the severity, there are several options, but we can discuss that when the time comes."

"When can I see him?"

"I'll have the nurse call down and let you know. Shouldn't be much longer. I'd prefer you only stay with him a few minutes, though. I want your father kept as quiet and undisturbed as possible. That means absolutely no stress. After you see him, I suggest you have your young man take you home to get some rest. We'll talk again tomorrow." The pager clipped to his pocket beeped. Dr. Bruley patted her on the shoulder and hurried away.

Tracy Lynn turned to Linc. "How am I supposed to guarantee that Daddy will stay calm? Especially after my baby news." She started to pace. "And what about the other thing—what you told him...?"

"I suppose we'll just have to pretend we're engaged—at least until the doc say he's in the clear."

"Engaged!" She glanced around and lowered her voice. "Who said anything about—"

"It's the next logical step when a man gets a woman pregnant."

"But you *didn't* get me pregnant!" If he intended to drive her crazy, it would be a very short trip.

"Your father thinks I did. He'll rest easier if he believes we're going to legitimize the baby and our relationship." Both his tone and his stance were so matter-of-fact, she was tempted to give him a shove just to get a reaction.

She speared her fingers through her hair, fisted the roots in her hands until the slight pain took away the very real urge to scream. What Linc said was true. In this instance, Daddy would expect a marriage to be on the agenda.

Who knew she'd find herself in a pretend engagement to Lincoln Slade?

"What if he takes longer to recover?" she asked, dropping her hands to her sides.

"You're borrowing trouble."

"I don't need to *borrow* any. You've managed to supply me with plenty." She realized her tone was less than charming. "I'm sorry. That sounded really ungrateful. I understand your intention. And it was sweet. I just hate for you to have to—"

"Babe."

"—stay here. And I—"

"Babe." He put his finger under her chin, effectively hushing her.

"What?" He was the only one who'd ever called her babe and gotten away with it. She'd considered the endearment slightly condescending to women. But with Linc, her reaction was just the opposite. He made the word sound caring. And darn it all, that gave her a thrill, made her feel special, exclusive.

"Quit worrying about me," he said. "I don't have anywhere else to be right now. So let's just chill and see what happens, okay?"

She shifted away from the finger that was now stroking her jaw. "Okay. Fine. And thank you," she added graciously. "But I still feel bad—even though a big part of this situation *is* your fault."

His lips quirked ever so slightly, but his eyes gave away nothing.

Sirens wailed as another ambulance pulled into the emergency bay, and she was aware of the smell of disinfectant. She was reminded all too well of the endless hours she'd spent at the hospital with her mother, the nights she'd go home reeking of odors she would forever associate with sickness and desperation—the desperation of family and friends clinging, often in vain, to hope.

"Ms. Randolph?"

Tracy Lynn whirled around as a volunteer in a blue jacket walked toward them.

"Yes," she answered. "I'm Tracy Lynn—Jerald Randolph's daughter."

‘‘We have your father in the third-floor coronary-care unit. Y’all can go on up now. I’ll take you.’’

Linc squeezed her shoulder. ‘‘I’ll be right here, babe.’’

‘‘Oh, you must be the beau,’’ the woman said, beaming at Linc. ‘‘I declare, y’all *do* make a beautiful couple! You can go up, too. Mr. Randolph is a mite agitated, and he’s asking for both of you.’’

Tracy Lynn met Linc’s gaze. A beautiful couple? Was her father already making assumptions and spreading the false news?

Good Lord, how much worse could this get?

Chapter Three

Tracy Lynn and Linc fell into step several paces behind their fleet-footed guide. The woman had to be eighty if she was a day, yet *Tracy Lynn* was the one about to break a sweat.

''I seem to recall you were in the drama class in high school,'' Linc murmured close to her ear. ''How would you rate your acting skills now?''

She gave him a blank look.

''Can you pretend we're engaged?'' he clarified. ''In love? Act as though we've slept together?''

His questions made her a nervous wreck. ''Um…I don't think we need to go overboard with the act.''

''Damn,'' he whispered. ''I suppose that means no kissing?''

He was teasing her. But she couldn't seem to communicate that to the butterflies fluttering in her stomach. More than once in her life, she'd fantasized about kissing Lincoln Slade.

Instead of answering him, she increased her pace and caught up with the volunteer, thanked the woman for the escort and assured her they wouldn't have any problems finding the third floor on their own.

A few minutes later, Tracy Lynn decided she might have been wiser to hang on to their guide. All the way up in the enclosed elevator, she was ultraaware of Linc by her side, his hands shoved in the pockets of his jeans.

She didn't exactly feel uncomfortable around him. Although this unwelcome attraction *was* a bit awkward. She didn't quite know how to define the feeling. Off balance? Weird? Completely crazy?

Often, she found herself trying hard not to look in his direction, not to let on she'd noticed him, for fear that he—or someone else—would catch her staring and read her curiosity, her interest.

And of course, trying to appear casual pretty much guaranteed her body language would project the exact opposite.

She'd felt a similar nervousness when he was a sullen teen, a year ahead of her in school. Even then, she'd worried that he could see her thoughts, sense the covert glances she sneaked his way, glances that had invariably been poorly timed and had slammed right into his.

Darn it all, he intrigued her, drew her, tempted her. Scared the living daylights out of her.

Was the temptation stronger because he'd been forbidden fruit? People tended to place more importance on what they couldn't have—or weren't allowed to have—than was actually warranted.

Or was it that Linc was the only man in her life

she wasn't sure of? The one whose emotions she'd never been able to figure out?

She wasn't used to feeling vulnerable, not knowing for certain where she stood with a guy, if she could even meet his expectations.

Good grief. Where had *that* little piece of insecurity come from? Usually, she realized, men were trying to meet *her* expectations.

For crying out loud. She was obsessing over Lincoln Slade, and it had to stop.

"If Daddy's asking for both of us, that must be a good sign," she said, her words loud in the silence of the elevator.

"Meaning he approves of me sleeping with his daughter?" He leaned a shoulder against the wall, his tone as nonchalant as his stance.

"I didn't sleep with you!"

"You just blew your line...Juliet," he drawled softly.

She gaped at him. "I hardly think the roles of Romeo and Juliet fit our situation."

"Close enough. Your daddy didn't approve of me ten years ago."

"Well, he apparently latched onto you quick enough when you legitimized my child!"

The elevator doors opened and she marched off, following the arrow aimed toward the coronary-care unit. She didn't need to look back to know Linc was behind her. She could *feel* him.

What in the world was the matter with her? Normally her emotions were as steady as an oak. Right now they ran more along the lines of a sapling in a gale-force wind, not at all like her. Pregnancy hormones, perhaps? Or simply that she'd had more than her share of upsets today.

She pressed a button on the wall and passed through the automatic doors admitting them to the CCU. The nurses' station was in the center of the ten-bed unit, affording them a view and quick access to all the patients.

Tracy Lynn's steps faltered when she spied her father through the opening in the drab green drapes that formed a U around his hospital bed.

A nasal cannula delivered oxygen through tubes that draped crookedly across his cheeks. Round patches sprouting wires that monitored his heart activity were stuck to his chest. He wore a faded blue hospital gown, which bunched around the cardiac apparatus. An IV was taped to his left forearm, a blood-pressure cuff wrapped around his right bicep.

She was dimly aware of Linc's steadying hand on her shoulder, the gentle squeeze of encouragement. She forced herself to step into the room, even as visions of her mother's lifeless body flashed through her mind. Her purse knocked against the guest chair and Jerald's eyes opened.

"Hey, Daddy," she said softly. "How're you feeling?"

"Like somebody parked a pickup on my chest." He peered around her. "No sense in standing out there in the middle of the room, Lincoln. Come in here and close the curtain so we can have some privacy.''

Tracy Lynn met Linc's gaze, recognizing the same resignation she knew her own must show. When he drew level with her, she slipped her hand in his with hardly a thought.

They'd agreed to pretend they were a couple. But for an instant, when his fingers twined with hers, and the side of her breast grazed his upper arm, she forgot all about pretense. This felt…real. And right.

Until her father spoke again.

''I expect you to do right by my daughter,'' he said to Linc. ''None of this long-engagement stuff now that the horse is already out of the barn. No sense giving folks *too* good a reason to count on their fingers when the baby's born. You get my drift?''

When Linc didn't answer, Tracy Lynn glanced at him. The two men were engaged in a stare-down, taking each other's measure in a silent battle of wills, evidently to determine who would win the position of control.

Linc's demeanor clearly indicated he took orders from no one.

Well, this was a fine time to toss a fly in the buttermilk, she thought. He'd placed himself in the hot seat with his hasty declaration, and now he'd turned mute. Had he forgotten about the no-stress mandate?

Jerald was the first to concede, thank goodness. Otherwise, they'd have been standing here all night.

''If something should happen to me, Tracy Lynn,''

he said, "I want to know you're settled with your husband and taken care of."

"Daddy, you just worry about getting well. I'm perfectly capable of taking care of myself. Besides, I wouldn't dream of getting married without you."

"There's no room for dreaming, girl. Randolphs don't go off havin' babies by themselves. First thing tomorrow morning, you be over at the courthouse. I'll call Judge Timber and let him know you're coming. He's a friend, he'll be discreet, and he'll cut a few inches off the red tape. You and Lincoln can be married by noon tomorrow."

Married? Tomorrow? Her gaze whipped to Linc's. *Now, what? This is only supposed to be pretend.* Do *something!*

The pressure cuff on her father's arm inflated, then slowly deflated as the electronic box on wheels measured his vitals. His blood pressure was 190 over 130.

Tracy Lynn's fingers tightened around Linc's hand, her nails digging into his palm. Linc squeezed her hand and let go, then moved closer to the bed.

"Leave the judge and the details to me, Jerald. You just concentrate on relaxing."

"I've been keeping an eye on you since you came back to town. I appreciate a man who betters himself." Her father paused, pulled oxygen through the tubes in his nose. "Takes a lot of grit. I'd have felt a little more kindly, though, if you'd stated your intentions toward my daughter sooner, instead of slipping around in secret."

Linc's features remained affable, but Tracy Lynn saw his shoulders tense. She stepped forward and eased her hand between his shoulder blades.

"Daddy, Linc learned about the baby the same time you did. We haven't even had a chance to discuss anything and—"

"Babe." Linc slid his arm around her waist, discreetly tipped his head toward the blood-pressure machine. "Let's talk about this later."

A nurse hurried into the room, cutting off any protest Jerald might have made. "Visiting time's up. *You,* Mr. Randolph, have orders to rest. And we need to get this pressure down. Open up. Nitroglycerine," she said as she popped a small pill under his tongue. She punched buttons on the machine and began to manually check his vitals. "I'm Ellie, the RN in this unit. You keep running up these numbers like this, sugar, and Dr. Bruley is going to accuse me of getting you all excited." She winked and leaned over him, pressing a stethoscope to his chest.

Tracy Lynn was close to tears. She'd never seen her strong father looking so weak and vulnerable. Her fear changed to a pang of censure when she saw the brief spark of masculine appreciation in his eyes as he gazed up at Ellie, who, at maybe forty-five, was trim and pretty. Mama had been dead for more than ten years, and there was no reason for Daddy to live like a monk. Still, the thought of him flirting or, worse, caring about another woman felt like a betrayal.

When Ellie straightened, Tracy Lynn lifted her father's hand, careful of the IV taped to his arm, and kissed his knuckles. "I'll see you in the morning, Daddy. You mind the doctors and nurses, now."

"Don't you worry," Ellie said. "We'll take good care of him."

Tracy Lynn nodded stiffly and allowed Linc to maneuver her toward the door.

"Bring me that paper we talked about," Jerald called cryptically. "You know what's at stake."

"Oh, no, you don't," Ellie said, misunderstanding. "There will be no paperwork done in my ward unless it involves your health, and I'm the one doing the writing. Now, shoo, you two, before Mayor Randolph gets it in his head to request a city council meeting."

Tracy Lynn waited until they'd reached the elevators before she spoke. She felt as though she was walking a high wire and the hole in the safety net below her kept getting bigger and bigger.

My gosh, her father had just insisted she get married! Tomorrow!

"Well, this is a fine how-do-you-do," Tracy Lynn said. "How did I manage to live with that man for nearly thirty years and not realize how adamantly he feels about public opinion? I never would've imagined I'd be an embarrassment to my family." An ache built in her chest. She'd been loved well all her life, and her father's judgment and disapproval felt like a rejection. It hurt.

"And to compound matters," she went on, "you've been dragged in with me. Some Pandora's box, huh? Open it a crack and now the whole lid has blown off. I'm afraid to wonder what'll happen next.''

He held the elevator door and she stepped in, still talking. ''Maybe I ought to leave town until the baby is born.''

''That won't make the problem go away, babe. The way I understand it, your father intends to run for the senate.''

She nodded. ''Yes.''

''And he's worried about his family—you—suffering because of campaign mud-slinging. But relocating won't prevent that. The opposition's dirt sleuth will still dig up every grain of information about you.''

''Artificial insemination is no big deal, for goodness' sake. It's not a scandal.'' Realizing the elevator hadn't moved, she reached around him and stabbed the ''lobby'' button.

''After the town blows it out of proportion, your means of conception will be a moot point,'' he said. ''The damage will have been done.''

''Why are you trying to talk me out of leaving?''

''Whether you stay or go is your call, babe. I'm just playing the devil's advocate. And I admit, I'm inclined to side with the devil on this one. Besides, the most important point at the moment is your dad's recovery, not his political aspirations.''

''So you're saying you're willing to go along with this charade? You're suggesting we actually get married?''

"My mother taught me to respect and protect a woman, and to be man enough to accept the responsibilities for the consequences of my actions. My lie got us into this, and I don't especially want to find myself staring down the barrel of your daddy's shotgun...or causing him permanent disability or death."

Death. The word was like an icy knife piercing her chest. The air around her seemed to thicken, become too dense to inhale. She felt smothered, panicked.

Linc slapped his palm against the red "stop" button and the elevator lurched to a halt. So did her heart.

"What in the world...?"

He cupped her face in his hands, bent his knees so that he was at eye level with her. "Look at me, Tracy Lynn."

She dragged her gaze from the elevator panel.

"I made a stupid call by saying I was your baby's father, but it's not the end of the world. We can deal with this. We'll only be going through the motions."

"You heard Daddy. He wants to see the marriage certificate. We can hold hands and call each other sweetie pie, but that piece of paper isn't easy to fake."

"So we'll get the certificate. Make the marriage legal—on *paper,*" he stressed. "The gossipmongers won't be able to light a good tongue fire, and your dad can relax and heal."

"Are you serious? Linc, I can't marry you."

''Sure you can. We're not talking about sharing a bed. Just an address. Temporarily.''

She studied him for a long moment, even though standing in an elevator suspended between floors wasn't entirely to her liking.

''What do you get out of the deal?'' she asked when he dropped his hands from her face. ''Why would you agree to tie yourself down this way?''

''If we're only acting, how can we be tied down?''

''You can't very well go out with other women if you marry me, for goodness' sake!'' She impatiently flicked her hair behind her ears. ''Oh, my gosh, I hadn't even thought about... Are you already in a relationship with someone?''

''My work doesn't leave a lot of time for a social life.''

''Now you sound like my father. Always thinking about work.''

''Keeps a roof over my head.''

''But does one man need such a big house?'' She'd seen the palatial ranch he'd built. ''I'd think as long as the rain's not dripping on you, that should be sufficient.''

''Strange, coming from an uptown woman who's used to living in mansions.''

''Mama and I would have been just as happy with a smaller house if it meant Daddy would've been home more.''

''Since my work is *at* my home, I think I'll refrain from tearing down walls. And we've veered off the subject. What I'd get out of a temporary marriage to you is—'' he paused as if considering ''—an interior decorator. I need someone to fix up my house, pick out furniture and stuff.''

''I'm not an interior decorator.''

''You don't need credentials to be good at something. You've got the know-how—my brother told me you helped him do up his house. I like your taste—classy, yet homey.''

''Oh. Well, thank you.''

''Besides,'' he continued, setting the elevator back in motion, ''we're both wealthy, so neither of us has to worry about the other making off with a bundle of cash and assets when the playacting is over.'' He shrugged. ''I don't see that we have an acceptable alternative here. Not with the shape your father's in. So we might as well quit talking about it and just do it.''

Tracy Lynn stared at Linc for a moment. She could see he was truly concerned—and prepared to take responsibility for his own part in her father's suffering.

She was worried sick about her father's health, too.

But marriage? To Lincoln Slade? In name only? Without sex?

Somebody ought to just shoot her now and get it over with.

Chapter Four

"Do you want to stop at Anna's and get something to eat?" Linc asked as he pulled his truck out of the hospital parking lot. Sunny's mother had bought Wanda's Diner and renamed it Anna's Café. It was the most popular gathering place in town.

"I'd just as soon go home, if you don't mind."

"No problem. What about your car?"

"It's at the house. I walked to the courthouse."

He nodded and flicked off the radio as she retrieved her cell phone from her purse. Tracy Lynn spent the ride back to Hope Valley calling her friends to update them on her father's condition. She didn't mention the marriage demand. Her thoughts were too scattered on that subject.

By the time they reached the Randolph mansion, night had fallen. The redbrick Colonial, with its forest-green shutters and white, three-story columns, loomed like the shadow of a hulking beast against the star-flecked sky. For the first time that Tracy Lynn could remember, not a single light illuminated the bevelled-pane windows.

Linc walked with her to the door, frowning when she pushed it open without using a key.

"I didn't expect to be gone long," she explained.

"You don't have live-in help? A cook or a housekeeper?" He reached around her to flick on the lights.

"Suelinda has Mondays off." She hesitated, looking inside, then back at him. "Do you want to come in? I could fix us some coffee. Or supper. The least I can do is feed you after all you've been through today on my behalf."

"I offered to buy dinner."

She moved into the foyer and set down her purse, leaving him to close the door behind them. "I didn't feel like being around a crowd of people." The phone rang and she slumped against the wall, closing her eyes.

"You going to answer that?"

"The machine will get it."

"It could be the hospital," he reminded her gently.

"I left them my cell phone number." The ringing stopped, but the recorder was in another part of the house, too far away to hear who was calling.

"When Mama was sick I spent most of my time on the telephone assuring everyone that she'd be just fine, that she was having a good day, and that between all of us, we could love her back into good health. She was so young, it seemed inconceivable that she wouldn't beat the cancer. I was so positive…and then I fielded those same calls all over again, having to explain that she'd died in my arms."

"Babe."

She opened her eyes, found him standing directly in front of her. "I don't know what to tell anybody, Linc…about Daddy. He might not be okay. And the thought terrifies me."

He pulled her against his chest and stroked her back through the soft knit of her sweater. Her hair smelled like orchids. He wanted to tell her not to worry…but he'd been there today, pumped on Jerald's chest when the man's heart had stopped beating. That wasn't a good thing.

"This morning, I was so excited about my baby," she whispered. "About finally giving Daddy a grandchild…"

"Shh." Linc was in over his head, didn't know what to say. He'd dealt with death, but not in the way Tracy Lynn had. He didn't know if he'd have been strong enough to hold his own mother as she slipped away.

She patted his chest as though he was the one in need of consoling, then stepped back, gathering her composure in one long, deep breath. "You poor thing. I'm sure you didn't wake up this morning expecting to get caught up in a Randolph family drama."

He shrugged. "Life was getting a little stale. A good drama now and again keeps me in shape. Why don't you point me in the direction of the kitchen, and I'll fix the coffee."

The phone started ringing again, and she groaned. "If I don't answer that, one of Storm's deputies will likely be knocking on my door, thinking I've gotten my foot stuck in the bathtub drain or something."

"Babe, if you get stuck in the bath, promise you'll let *me* come to your rescue."

She laughed and ducked her head. "You've rescued above and beyond the call of duty today. Change the beverage menu to wine. I'll probably need it. Kitchen's through there." She gestured toward the arched doorway of the living room, then sat on a dinky piece of furniture—part sofa, part table—and lifted the telephone receiver.

Linc found the kitchen easily. The Randolph mansion was large, but the place he'd built out on his and his brother's property was even more massive.

He hadn't been consciously competitive when he'd altered the plans the architect had presented, but now he realized he had increased the square footage of his ranch for the purpose of outdoing the Randolphs. A subtle statement that he could never again be judged and found lacking—at least not when it came to money and power.

Never again would he feel trapped in poverty, suffer looks of pity or scorn from haughty people who had no idea what it was like to go to bed hungry or be forced to rummage through garbage cans just to survive. Never again would he be bullied...or beaten.

The realization that he'd used the Randolphs as a success yardstick annoyed him. He'd come home to Hope Valley hoping to put the past behind him, to see if he could resolve his feelings about the deceased, abusive father he hated and a town that held mostly bad memories.

He'd given himself six months. Four had already elapsed, and not once had he been able to step foot in the shed-row stable behind his brother's house. He'd told himself that was merely because he was too busy building his own place.

Which was a lie.

Every morning he awoke in this town, the banked rage dogged him. And visiting the scene of his worst nightmare could do one of two things—give him peace…or break him.

He hadn't decided if the risk was worth taking.

He rolled his shoulders, shook away the tension, then put on a pot of coffee, poured a glass of apple juice for Tracy Lynn and retraced his steps to the foyer.

With the telephone receiver pressed to her ear, she accepted the stemmed glass and took a sip. She frowned and looked at the beverage. He watched her eyes widen as understanding dawned. She'd asked for wine and he'd given her juice.

One of them had remembered she was pregnant.

Her expression went from surprise to dewy-eyed gratitude as she mouthed a heartfelt thank-you.

For an instant, longing nearly buckled his knees. She was the image of everything he'd ever wanted in a woman.

Her blond hair hung silky and straight to her shoulders. Eyes the color of Texas bluebonnets caressed him even as she continued her conversation on the phone. Her soft sweater skimmed her breasts, rested against her flat stomach, barely touching the low waist of her figure-hugging black slacks. She wore a lapis lazuli ring on her right hand—her birthstone, he knew, because his was the same—and small diamond studs in her ears.

She looked elegant, yet relaxed and approachable, the type of woman who'd welcome a man's hands in her hair, wouldn't pitch a fit if he had a mind to mess her up a bit.

God help him, he'd offered to marry her in order to smooth her relationship with her father. Yet instead of feeling forced by circumstances he'd had a big hand in creating, he found himself looking forward to spending time with her under the same roof. His roof. Even if he *did* have to keep his hands off her.

WHEN TRACY LYNN FINISHED her phone call, Linc cajoled her into eating one of the ham sandwiches he'd fixed, then he lit the logs in the living room fireplace while she went upstairs to change her clothes. He knew she was beat, but he was reluctant to leave her alone just yet.

She came into the room carrying a bottle of wine and wearing roomy sweats that still managed to look sexy.

"Do you want some wine?" she asked, holding up the bottle. "Just because I can't imbibe doesn't mean you shouldn't enjoy it."

"I don't drink alcohol."

''Oh.''

''Weird quirk,'' he explained. ''Comes from having an old man who wouldn't know sober if it shook his hand.'' He patted the sofa cushion next to him. ''Come here.''

She hesitated for a moment, then set the wine and stemmed glass on the coffee table and sat next to him, inhaling swiftly when he pulled her legs onto his lap.

''Lie back,'' he said, positioning a decorative pillow against the sofa's arm behind her head. Her exhalation ended on a moan when he began to massage her feet.

''Oh, that feels so good.''

His body responded to her words, and to the press of her heels against his crotch. He shifted his thigh so neither of them would end up feeling embarrassed.

For long moments, the only sound in the room was the crackle of the fire.

''You didn't come to your father's funeral,'' she said.

He glanced at her, sorry he'd even brought up the subject of his father. ''How do you know? Were you there?''

''Yes.''

That surprised him. ''Why?''

''Out of respect.''

He gave a derisive snort. ''I didn't have any respect for Russell Slade. Change the subject, babe.''

''Sorry. I didn't mean to hit a sore spot.'' She flexed her foot in his hand. ''I called the hospital while I was upstairs. Ellie said the doctor was in again to see Daddy. He's not settling and they want his blood pressure to come down before they do the angiogram in the morning. I just know he's lying there letting his mind run away with him.''

''He'll feel more at ease tomorrow. What's next after the angiogram?''

''Ellie's pretty sure the doctor will opt for bypass surgery if there's blockage. *If* they think he's strong enough to survive the operation.''

Linc ran through a list of things he needed to accomplish by morning. Getting married wasn't normally an overnight process. But in small towns, and especially when someone had a direct connection to the judge, as Jerald did, rules could be bent.

Something inside him went bump when he thought of the step he was about to take. He'd gambled more, though, on the purchase of a champion Thoroughbred with a history of premature foaling. That, too, had been a temporary contract. The owner, a friend of his, had been facing bankruptcy, yet still held a fierce belief his mare would eventually come through for him. Linc had lent his own resources, providing the time his friend needed to gain his financial feet and for the mare to foal successfully.

Although he didn't think Tracy Lynn would appreciate being compared to a horse, their temporary marriage agreement wasn't that much different.

He ran his hands up her legs, took her right hand where it rested on her abdomen and began to massage her palm and fingers.

"Do you want me to hang out with you while your dad has the procedure? Or just meet you someplace for the ceremony?"

She tugged back on her hand, but he didn't let go. "You don't have to be there. And…shouldn't we wait on the civil service? Maybe Daddy will be stronger tomorrow and I can just tell him the truth about the baby."

"Maybe. Then again maybe not. Seems to me that telling him now will just give him a new set of worries. He didn't sound too keen on the idea of single parenthood."

"I never knew Daddy was so stuck in the Dark Ages. Why can't he just not worry about me? I'm almost thirty!"

"Be glad you have the kind of father who *does* worry about you."

She closed her fingers around his. "Oh, Linc. I'm sorry."

"Nothing to be sorry for." He quickly shifted the topic. "Look, let's just keep things as is. I'll arrange for the judge to meet us at the hospital around noon or before, depending on his schedule. That'll give your father time to get through his tests and rest up. We can have the ceremony right there in his room. It'll ease his mind."

She pulled her hand back to push herself into a sitting position, and her ring came off in his palm. "This all seems so extreme."

He studied the bright blue stone, slipping it on and off his pinkie. "Consider it an act of kindness—a good deed. We're eliminating a point of stress so a man has the best chance of healing, and I'm getting my house decorated. Nothing's permanent. When the time comes, I'll have my attorneys take care of the annulment—or a divorce if that'll look better. There's nothing scandalous about a politician's daughter being divorced.''

''There's nothing scandalous about her having a baby through anonymous donor insemination, either.''

''No, but that's easier to twist out of proportion. Besides, I've been a bachelor for so long I could use a trial run to see how I like family life. Jack and Sunny make it look pretty good.''

''You want me to prepare you for the woman you'll eventually fall in love with and marry?''

He shrugged and slipped the ring back on her finger. ''I figure you're the best test I could have. You're a girly girl, and I'm an outdoorsman. If I can cohabitate peacefully with you, I can live with anyone.''

She whacked him with the sofa pillow. ''Thanks a lot.''

He grinned. ''Hey, I've already heard the story about you knocking down a tent over a teeny spider.''

''It wasn't teeny. It was nearly a tarantula. And I was twelve at the time.''

''You're still a city girl.''

''There are advantages to city girls.'' She flicked her hair off her shoulder. ''We have impeccable fashion and decorating tastes that obviously impress even you country boys.''

His lips twitched. Her cheeks were pink and passion sparked in her blue eyes, instead of sadness.

''Think you can manage living way out on a horse farm with a country boy?''

''I guess we'll soon find out.''

''Guess we will. Do you want me to stay tonight, or will you be okay on your own?''

Her cheeks colored, as though she was actually thinking about him spending the night—and doing much more than sleeping.

''I'll be fine. You can just meet me at the hospital tomorrow.'' She stood and gathered his coat from the mahogany hall tree. The perfect hostess, even while wearing sweats that bagged at the knees and butt.

Frigid air swirled in when he opened the door. He knew he should go, but he was suddenly reluctant. She was looking up at him, her lips slightly parted. It would be so easy to lower his head and kiss her. He wanted to in the worst way, had an idea she'd invite him back in for more. There was definite chemistry going on between them.

But answering that invitation would be taking unfair advantage.

So, instead, he simply stroked her warm cheek. ''Try not to worry, okay? Everything will work out fine.''

TRACY LYNN WASN'T SURE what to wear to a hospital wedding. Or if there would even be a wedding.

For all she knew, her father could have rallied overnight and had a total change of heart about her condition.

Regardless, she figured she ought to be prepared, and finally settled on a simple wool skirt in winter white and a soft blue sweater.

The angiogram procedure didn't take long, but by the time the doctor came out to report that there was severe blockage in both ventricles of the heart and bypass surgery was urgent, Tracy Lynn's nerves were a wreck. Accepting the inevitable, she went down to the hospital cafeteria, bought a bottle of fruit juice, then sat down at a table on the outside patio, took out her cell phone and punched in the number for Becca's Attic.

"Hey, it's me," she said when Becca answered.

"How's your dad?"

"They've scheduled him for bypass surgery. The doctor wants to wait a couple of days, whip him into a little better shape before they put him under the knife."

"Oh, Tracy Lynn, it'll be all right. He's a tough old cuss. And not that old, anyway."

"Tough old cuss is right. He's backed me into a corner, and...I'm going to marry Linc."

"What! When?"

"Sometime this morning, I guess. Whenever he and Judge Timber get here."

"You're getting married at the hospital?"

"Daddy is in a state. He wants to see the marriage certificate. Linc thinks if Daddy witnesses the wedding firsthand, it'll put his mind at rest. Meanwhile, will you call Sunny and Donetta for me? Just to keep everyone in the loop."

"Of course. I'll close up the shop, and I'm sure Donetta can rearrange her clients, and Sunny can—"

"No. Becca, it's just a quick exchange of 'I do's.' If we have a big crowd here, it'll call attention to us, and people will start questioning the baby—which we have to keep quiet about for the next month or so. I just wanted you all to know beforehand."

"Trace, you can't get married without us!"

"I'm not…I mean, it's not a *real* marriage. Linc is just helping me out of a tricky situation."

"What will you do after the ceremony? Are you going home? Or to Linc's house?"

"I'll be staying at Linc's—so things look normal." She sighed, nerves churning in her stomach. "I'll have to stop by my house and get some clothes, I suppose."

"We can help you with that," Becca said.

"Thanks. But not today, okay? I figure I'll just pack a small suitcase for the time being. If Daddy comes home, he'll need someone there to help, so no sense moving everything."

"*When* he comes home, Trace," Becca said. "And I still think you should let us come to the ceremony. You've dreamed about your wedding day since we were kids."

"I know. Maybe someday I'll find the real thing. Then the three of you can make plans and annoy me with your organizational skills..." She paused while Becca snorted a laugh—Tracy Lynn was clearly the one who had the organizational skills. "And we'll all walk down the church aisle like we always talked about, and—oh!"

Linc was standing behind her shoulder.

"I've gotta go, Becca. I'll talk to you later. Don't worry."

She disconnected the phone and stood up, smoothing her damp palms on her skirt. "I didn't realize you were here."

He wore a pair of dark jeans with a white shirt tucked in at the waist and a brown leather jacket. His suede Stetson was the color of rich chocolate that matched his boots.

"The judge is up in your dad's room," he said, his gray-blue eyes watchful. "Ellie already filled me in on the test results and surgery schedule. You ready to do this?"

Her hands trembled as she stuffed her cell phone in her purse. "If you are?" The answer came out as a question.

He took her hand and drew it through the crook of his elbow. "Let's go get married."

She was as nervous as a painted lady at a prayer meeting. Thank goodness this wedding *wasn't* taking place at church.

Minutes later they were standing with Judge Timber by her father's bed in the CCU. Linc drew the curtains around them for privacy. Jerald's eyes filled with tears.

Tracy Lynn had to swallow back her own tears. And in that moment, she knew what they were doing was right—even if it was a lie.

"Don't start, Daddy," she said softly. "You'll get me going."

"It's just that I always thought your mama would be here with me when you got married."

Tracy Lynn swallowed. "I think she's watching."

The judge retrieved a book he'd set on the tray table, then paused when the curtains behind them were snatched open. Ellie bustled in, pushing an IV pole. She stopped.

"You all look so serious in here. Am I interrupting?"

Linc pulled the drapes closed again. "If you've got a few minutes, you can stand in as our witness. Tracy Lynn and I decided to move up our wedding date. I know Tracy—" he paused and pressed a kiss to her temple "—and with Jerald scheduled for surgery and then his recovery time, she'd make herself nuts trying to plan a wedding and worry about her dad, too. So we're eloping." He winked. "Right here to Mercy General."

Ellie chuckled. "Well, I'd be honored." She checked her watch, then stood at the head of the bed by Jerald's side.

"We'll be quick," Linc said, looking toward the judge as though to make sure he understood.

Judge Timber nodded.

Tracy Lynn was still trying to regain her breath after that gentle kiss.

"If you two will face each other and join hands," the judge said, "we'll get started. Lincoln, do you come to this union of your own free will, and with the intention of being faithful in marriage to Tracy Lynn as long as you live?"

"I do." His voice was strong, causing Tracy Lynn's heart to thud even harder.

"And you, Tracy Lynn, do you come to this union of your own free will, and with the intention of being faithful in marriage to Lincoln as long as you live?"

She nodded. "Yes. I mean, I do."

Linc smiled at her and squeezed her hands, which were shaking like mad. So far she hadn't said anything to cause a lightning bolt to strike her down. The judge hadn't actually said she had to stay married as long as she lived, just to be faithful in the marriage. And that would be easy.

The pressure in her chest eased slightly.

"Lincoln, please repeat the following after me..."

In a strong voice that held her spellbound, his eyes steady on hers, Linc followed the judge's lead. "I, Lincoln Thomas Slade, take you, Tracy Lynn, to be my lawfully wedded wife. I promise from this day forward to be your faithful husband, for better or worse, for richer, for poorer, in sickness and in health, I will love and cherish you, as long as I live."

The sincerity of his tone made her feel faint. This didn't sound like pretend. She could almost believe that he did, and *would,* love her as he vowed.

When it was her turn, her voice shook. This time

she couldn't rationalize away the lifelong vow, and she didn't even begin to try.

Because at that moment, she wanted nothing more than to have Lincoln Slade look at her just this way...for the rest of her life.

Stunned by that realization, she didn't realize for a moment that the judge had spoken and Linc was reaching in his pocket.

He took her left hand and slipped a ring on her finger. An eternity band.

Her dizziness grew.

"In pledge of the vow of marriage made between us," he said, "I offer you this ring."

She stared at the circle of diamonds on her finger. She hadn't expected...how had he found time to get her a ring? She should have reciprocated. As the diamonds winked up at her, a memory flashed in her head: a ring, with a small horseshoe of diamonds, tucked away in her ballerina jewelry box beneath a stack of camisoles in her dresser drawer.

"Babe," Linc said softly.

She looked up. As her brain scrambled to rewind, she vaguely recalled the judge pronouncing them husband and wife, and...

Her heart leaped right into her throat.

With utter tenderness, he framed her face in his hands and kissed her.

Chapter Five

The kiss was fleeting, yet it conveyed a world of tenderness. If Linc hadn't been holding her, she might have dropped right to her knees.

Whenever her fantasies had run amok and Lincoln Slade had played the starring role, she'd never imagined a kiss could make her feel so much. Joy, sadness, confusion. Love.

She stepped back and cleared her throat, glanced at her father. A single tear tracked from the corner of Jerald's left eye. How could she hold his high-handedness against him when this marriage obviously meant so much to his peace of mind? He wasn't an overbearing father. Just a worried one, set in the ways of his upbringing.

She should have considered that before she'd decided to have a child on her own—without discussing it with her father first. Oh, how she'd miscalculated on this one.

And now, after years of searching for the right man, after not finding him and giving up, Linc Slade had reentered her life. And something deep inside her regretted, for an instant, that she hadn't waited just a little longer before seeking out a doctor to help her complete her dream.

"I'll need you both to sign the certificate," Judge Timber said.

Tracy Lynn signed the document, then watched while Linc and Ellie—as witness—did the same.

"Well, that's it, I guess." She sat down in the guest chair while Ellie finished hanging the IV bag she'd brought in, and Linc walked the judge out to pay for his services.

"Congratulations," Ellie said. "And thanks for letting me be a part of your happy day. I think it's special that you changed your plans this way for your father." She exchanged a look with Tracy Lynn that indicated she knew what was behind the hurry—fear that Jerald wouldn't make it through his surgery.

But that was only part of it. The other part—the baby she wanted so fiercely—had to remain secret until an appropriate amount of time had passed for them as husband and wife.

On her way out, Ellie hugged Linc, who was returning. He stopped next to Tracy Lynn's chair, resting his hand lightly on her shoulder. Just that simple touch made her pulse jump.

"Thank you both for doing this for me," Jerald said, looking at Linc, then at Tracy Lynn, his voice still weak. "I know it's not what you'd dreamed your wedding would be like, honey."

"As long as you're here, Daddy, that's all that matters."

Ellie came back through the curtains dragging another chair for Linc.

"No need for that," Jerald said. "You two go on now and get started on your honeymoon. No sense in hanging around this place."

"We've got plenty of time for...um, the honeymoon," Tracy Lynn said, though she noticed that Linc didn't sit. She figured theirs would be the most platonic honeymoon in history—and she'd be the most frustrated bride.

"Truth is, honey, I'm pretty worn out. I think I'd just like to rest now."

"You can go ahead and sleep." She turned to Linc. "I'll stay here with Daddy if you want to go."

"No," Jerald said. "You two git. I don't need anyone watching me sleep or hovering over my bed. I'll feel like I've got to stay awake and be sociable."

Linc urged her to her feet. "We'll call and check on you later." He shook hands with Jerald, then stepped back so Tracy Lynn could lean down and kiss her father.

"Bye, Daddy." She adjusted the blanket, pulling it up to his chest. Kissing him again, she said, "Rest. I'll see you later."

"Not tonight, girl. I mean it."

She glanced at the blood-pressure machine, then back at her father. Arguing would only increase his stress level. "You're a stubborn, bossy man, but I love you."

Jerald waved and Linc steered her out of the room,

holding her hand in his. All the way to the elevator, he kept her close.

She was grateful for his steadiness. The morning had taken a lot out of her. First waiting for the angiogram results, finding out her father would undergo open heart surgery, then the marriage ceremony.

And that kiss. Dear heaven, that kiss.

The minute the elevator doors closed, he let go of her hand and abruptly moved away.

Disappointment dredged a path from the pit of her stomach to the base of her throat. She'd almost gotten caught up in the event, almost convinced herself this was real.

Reality check, Tracy Lynn.

The air grew rife with tension as they both stared at the lighted number panel—typical elevator behavior of perfect strangers who dared not look in each other's direction for fear they'd have to speak.

This was ridiculous.

"So what's next?" she asked, determined not to let her emotions show.

He shrugged, still staring straight ahead. "I suppose we head for my place. I can give you a tour, get your input on what kind of decorating it needs."

"Maybe we should stop by my house first so I can get some clothes? I mean…I'm staying at your place, right?"

"That's the plan," he said, finally turning toward her. "Especially since you still live with your father."

"Is that a criticism?"

''No.'' He raked a hand through his hair. ''Look, I'm walking blind through this just like you are.''

''Are you sorry?''

The elevator doors opened to the main lobby. Without answering, he slid his arm around her waist.

Tracy Lynn stiffened.

''Snuggle up, babe. Gotta keep up appearances.''

She put her arm around his waist purely for self-preservation. Otherwise, the awkward gait might land her flat on her face. ''No one in the lobby knows we're married,'' she whispered.

''They will by tomorrow's paper. You want one of these folks reading about us and thinking back to seeing us get off the elevator looking as though we'd never met?''

He was the one acting as if she had girl cooties. ''How's the paper going to know?''

''I'm going to call them. Quickest way to get the news out so that when it's announced we're expecting, no one'll be surprised.''

''Are you sure that's such a good idea?''

''Ashamed of your husband?'' he asked.

''Darn it, Linc! Why do you insist on painting me as a snob?'' She was teetering on the edge of a crying jag. ''This was *your* idea.''

When they stepped through the automatic door into the chilly afternoon air, he swung her around and pulled her against his chest, his hand on the back of her head.

''I apologize—for that comment,'' he clarified. ''I'm being an ass, and I have no idea why.''

"I do," she said, her voice muffled in the front of his white shirt. "You've just been railroaded into marriage."

"That was my choice. And to answer your question, no, I'm not sorry." He pulled the edges of his jacket around her when she shivered. "Where's your coat?"

"In my car. I forgot to put it on." He started to remove his jacket, but she stopped him. "I'm fine, Linc. I'll just have to take it off again in a few minutes. I hate to drive with a coat on."

"Then let's get you inside your car." He tucked her under his arm and shielded her from the chill wind as they walked through the parking lot to her flashy red Mustang convertible.

"I'll follow you to your place, then we'll head on over to mine. Sound like a plan?"

She nodded, then looked up at him. "This is going to work, isn't it? I mean, we did the right thing, didn't we?"

His gaze lingered on her mouth for a long moment. "You're just changing residences for a while, babe. It's not that big a deal."

"It *feels* like a big deal. I've never been married before."

"Neither have I. So I guess we'll muddle through together. As soon as your dad's on his feet, we'll come clean. I'd planned to go back to Dallas some time after the first of the year. If need be, we can use that time to ease folks into accepting that the marriage didn't work out."

She rested her forehead against his chest. "I never thought I'd be discussing divorce on my wedding day."

With a finger under her chin, he lifted her head. "Then let's not." He opened her car door. "Try to keep the shiny side up, speed racer."

She tsked and slid into the driver's seat of her Mustang. "Why does everyone pick on my driving? I hardly ever get a speeding ticket."

"That's because one of your best friends is married to the sheriff."

Rolling her eyes, she shut the car door, closing out the chill, and watched him amble over to his truck.

Her husband.

He made her pulse race with only a look.

And now she was going home to pack her clothes and move in with him.

Lord, what had she done?

LINC CHECKED HIS REARVIEW mirror as he drove beneath the canopy of live oaks and pulled up in front of his house. Tracy Lynn's red Mustang was right on his tail, her blond head bobbing to the beat of whatever was playing on the car's stereo.

His wife.

Man alive, living in close proximity to this woman and keeping his hands to himself was going to be pure torture. She had a body that wouldn't quit and a face that made a man want to just sit and look at her for a good long while.

But she was sweet, too, and fun. Even finding herself in the midst of a grave situation, hanging out at hospitals and all, she could still laugh—and make *him* laugh, too.

He realized that he was looking forward to showing her his world—the house, the horses…he wished like crazy he could do more than show her his bedroom.

Not watching where he was going, he nearly rear-ended his brother's pickup. "What the…? Bad time for a visit, bro," he muttered.

Looking around, he saw Donetta's red Tahoe, Storm's cruiser with the county sheriff's emblem on the side, and Becca Sue's dinky Volkswagen.

He parked, hefted Tracy Lynn's suitcases from the bed of the truck and waited for her to join him. Before they'd left her father's house, she'd changed into a pair of body-hugging jeans that made her legs look a mile long, and a tight little top that played peek-a-boo with her navel every time she moved.

For his own peace of mind, he wondered if he could talk her into leaving on the denim jacket once they got inside, then decided it didn't much matter. He could still see smooth skin with or without the jacket.

"Welcome to the south half of the Forked S ranch," he said when she reached his side. "Looks like your sweetheart pals are helping themselves to my new house for a get-together."

Tracy Lynn sighed. "I told Becca to spread the word about our marriage. I didn't expect them to rush right over."

"Guess I won't need to run the article in the paper, after all."

"Daddy might feel better if we made a formal announcement. I'll ask him later, okay? Then we can decide."

"Babe, stand still. There's a bee buzzing around you. Seems to think your hair is a flower."

She froze as if he'd told her a rattler was circling her feet. A split second later, she flailed her arms wildly, ducked, then gave a tiny shriek and nearly body-slammed him. Grabbing his jacket, she whirled him around, using him as a shield between her and the poor insect.

"Why didn't you tell me?"

"I just *did* tell you."

"Is it gone?" she asked.

"Yep. You scared him pretty good."

She let go of his jacket and gave his back a light thump. Straightening the hem of her top, she lifted her chin. "Some people are allergic to bee stings, you know."

Ah, hell. "Are you?"

"No. But I could have been. You should think about that before making fun."

He chuckled. "I have a feeling you're going to be quite entertaining."

"Entertainment is my forte. And isn't that lucky, seeing as we're apparently about to host our very first party together." She grinned at him, deliberately misunderstanding his comment. "Shall we go greet our guests?"

''I imagine that'd be the proper thing to do.'' Linc stepped ahead of her through the double-door entry, and his chocolate Lab trotted out to meet them.

''Oh, sweetheart,'' Tracy Lynn crooned.

Linc's heart jumped and his head whipped around in surprise. He felt like a fool when he realized she was talking to his dog.

''That's Starbuck,'' he said. ''Better known as Buck.''

Kneeling, she lavished Buck with hugs and pats as though this was a reunion instead of an introduction.

Before he could set down the luggage, Sunny's huge, goofy-looking hound came around the corner, slipping and sliding over the tile entry floor like Scooby-Doo on roller skates executing four-legged splits.

''Heads up!'' Linc warned.

''Simba!'' Sunny yelled at the same time. The dog, which was nearly the size of a month-old colt, skidded to a stop, but momentum worked against him and he kept right on sliding. Buck managed to jump clear of the canine menace, but Tracy Lynn ended up on her behind.

Linc abandoned the luggage and reach down a hand to help her up, snapping his fingers at both dogs and pointing in the opposite direction. Well trained, the animals gave them room.

''You okay, babe?'' he asked.

Tracy Lynn laughed. ''Fine. I'm used to Simba's exuberance.'' She glanced past him. ''Hey, y'all.''

Linc looked back at his sister-in-law, who'd been joined by Jack and their nine-year-old daughter, Tori, plus Donetta and Storm, and Becca Sue. Simba and Buck, tongues lolling, were sitting politely beside Tori. A moment later, Beau Thompson ambled into the entry hall, followed by Cora Harriet.

"What in tarnation is all the hollering about? Oh. The newlyweds are here." Tall and skinny, gray-haired and bowlegged as a barrel hoop, Beau frowned and wiped his hands on the apron he wore over blue jeans and a snap-front shirt.

Semiretired now, Beau had been the number-one cowboy on the Forked S for as long as Linc could remember. Nowadays Beau spent his time in the kitchen over at Jack's place, arguing with the housekeeper, Cora, over which one of them was the boss.

"Well, don't just stand there draggin' yer rope," Beau said. "Get on in here and eat some of this food Becca Sue's had me fixin'."

Cora whacked Beau on the arm. "You could at least ask after Tracy Lynn's relations before you go braying like a sore-headed mule!"

"Beg pardon, Miss Tracy Lynn. How's that daddy of yours holding up?"

"Ornery as ever. The tests show he has serious blockage in his arteries. The doctor wants to do a quadruple bypass in a couple of days—*if* they feel he's strong enough to tolerate the surgery."

"Well, don't you worry none," Beau said. "That Jerald's got plenty of fur on his brisket. He'll come through jest fine. Now, can we get this here show on the road?''

''I hadn't realized we were having a party,'' Linc said. He looked at his brother. ''Did we get our wires crossed on the reason for the occasion?''

Beau answered before Jack could. ''Boy, it don't matter if a neighbor's steer wandered over jest to drink out of the trough. Women folk'll use any excuse for socializing. Now, make yourself useful and put your wife's belongings someplace other than in the dadgum doorway where a body's likely to trip over them.-''

''Language!'' Cora scolded.

Beau rolled his eyes. ''Beg pardon, Miss Victoria,'' he said glancing at Tori. Turning back to Cora, he squinted at her. ''Though, I'd like to know what book says *dadgum* is a cuss word.''

''*My* book does, you old goat,'' Cora answered, perching her hands on her hips.

Obviously realizing he was outgunned, he turned his sights back on Linc. ''Fan the fat, man. There's work to be done. Jack and Storm managed to get that fancy barbecue of yours fired up, but I imagine they could do with a few pointers so they don't go ruining my spareribs.''

''A man ought not to get bossed around in his own home,'' Linc grumbled, feeling a smile tug at his mouth when Beau just squinted his eyes again and headed back to the kitchen.

Sunny stepped forward and plopped a straw cowboy hat on Tracy Lynn's head. Attached to the hatband was a white fluff of netting.

A wedding veil.

Man alive. They were having a wedding reception.

And when it was over, he couldn't even look forward to taking his bride to bed.

Since Tracy Lynn was being whisked away by the Sweethearts, he carried her bags upstairs and put them in the spare bedroom, glad to see that Jack had brought over a bed and dresser.

The house was sparsely furnished, and the only other sleeping accommodations were in the master bedroom—and sharing that with Tracy Lynn wasn't part of the deal. So, he'd had to call Jack and ask him to haul a mattress and box spring out of the attic in the old homestead.

He traced one of the bluebonnets on the quilt that either Jack or Sunny had spread over the bed. His mother's work. Countless nights he'd watched as Doris Slade had hand-stitched intricate patterns on material that had ended up on their beds, been given as gifts or sold at church auctions.

A wave of sadness caught him by surprise. He missed his mother's sweet voice, her gentle touch. He wondered what she would have thought about his marriage to Tracy Lynn, wondered if she would have seen more in his motives than he wanted to admit to.

He'd been sixteen when his mother had died—no, when his father had *murdered* her. He balled his hand into a fist, felt a twinge in his back, as though the scars had opened up.

In Linc's mind, when a man got blind, stinking drunk and plowed the truck into a tree, killing his passenger, that was murder.

But Russell Slade had known how to get around the law. Linc still believed his father had slept all night in that wrecked pickup hidden in the trees, giving the alcohol level in his blood enough time to drop before he'd hiked home to call the authorities.

Swearing, Linc forced the images from his mind, whirled and left the room. Music played on the stereo downstairs, and voices rose in laughter, reminding him there was a reception being held in honor of his pretend marriage.

As he reached the bottom of the stairs, the doorbell rang. He crossed the foyer and opened the door. Anna Carmichael, along with her mother, Birdie Alder, and Donetta's grandmother, Betty Wagner—better known as Grandma Birdie and Grammy Betty—stood on the porch, each holding a covered dish. Millicent Lloyd, the blue-haired lady who owned half the town, was making her way up the steps behind them.

"Goodness me," Birdie said. "I believe we ought to have a talk with the Man upstairs, don't you think, Betty? We got gypped, because He sure didn't make boys this handsome when we were girls."

"Mother!" Anna exclaimed. "Hush up and behave."

"I'm of a mind to agree with Birdie," Betty commented. "Hello, Linc. Congratulations."

Instead of responding verbally, he merely tipped

his head in acknowledgment. He wasn't sure how to react to the foursome, wondered if they knew the true situation. He'd have to get Jack off to the side and find out what was what.

"Are y'all going to stand on the porch all afternoon?" Millicent Lloyd demanded, skirting the group. "My hot tamales are turning to icicles. Step aside, Lincoln, and let's have a look at this king-size manor you got the whole town speculatin' on."

"Good gawd, Millie. There you go, airing your mind before any of us has had a chance to even cuss and discuss." Birdie's admonishment didn't hold an ounce of credibility since she was right on Millicent's heels, trying to see inside the house past the woman's blue hair. "Gol, would you get a load of that chandelier. Imagine if it fell down. It'd squash you flat as a bug."

Millicent rolled her eyes at Birdie, sniffed and headed in the direction of the kitchen as if she'd drawn up the architectural floor plan herself. Betty gave the area beneath the light fixture a wide berth.

Bemused, Linc shut the door behind Anna, who apologized profusely for the other three women.

What the hell had happened to his solitary, calm, *sane* lifestyle?

AFTER EATING WAY TOO MUCH food, Tracy Lynn took her herbal tea and followed Becca, Sunny and Donetta through the archway that separated the great room from the slightly smaller living room. Having her friends here to act as a buffer had taken away the anxiety of being alone with Linc, given her a chance to find her balance.

Typical of a couples get-together, the men migrated to one end of the room and the women to the other. The older generation—with the exception of Beau—had remained in the kitchen to tidy up and discuss the corns on Miz Lloyd's feet, each woman having an opinion on the best way to deal with the pain.

Tracy Lynn remembered Donetta likening the grandmas and Miz Lloyd to the Ya-Ya sisters. She was starting to agree.

"How long do you think it'll be before your dad's able to handle the truth about you and Linc?" Donetta asked.

"I don't know," Tracy Lynn said. "That's what makes this whole ordeal so scary. I'm used to calling the shots, knowing what I'll be doing at any given time. Right now, I don't even know what bed I'm sleeping in."

Becca, of course, had to pounce. "The master bedroom is always a good choice. Especially if there's a hottie like Linc in there."

Donetta flicked her wild, curly red hair over her shoulder. "Becca Sue, you need a boyfriend. You practically pushed me into bed with Storm, and now you're egging on Tracy Lynn with Linc."

"Just because I'm a romantic doesn't mean I need a boyfriend," Becca said with a scowl. "Besides, wasn't I right about you and Storm? And I happen to have two eyes in my head, and I can *see* that there's chemistry between Tracy and Linc."

"Would you two stop talking about me as if I'm not in the room?" Tracy Lynn said, huffing out a breath. "Stress is not good for pregnant women—Donetta, that includes you, so behave."

"Yes, ma'am." Donetta saluted smartly, grinning. Simba cut a clumsy path through the living room with Buck and Tori hot on his heels. Probably because Simba had stolen the Lab's chew toy, and Tori was a stickler for fairness.

"You can get out of this situation, Tracy Lynn," Sunny said, her voice sincere and soft. "I know your dad put pressure on you, but he'll come around. He can't stay mad at you for more than five minutes, and the last thing he'd ever want is for you to be living with someone who makes you uncomfortable."

"Linc doesn't make me uncomfortable—at least not in the sense you seem to be intimating. He tempts me something fierce, and I have to keep reminding myself not to go overboard, to protect myself from a big letdown. Still, I'm annoyed that it takes marriage to make me and my child legitimate. Honestly! I *chose* single motherhood."

"Yes, but that wasn't your first choice," Becca reminded her. "Over the years, you've dated enough men to outfit an army—with the express purpose of finding the right one."

"Yes, well, I didn't find him, did I."

"Are you sure?" Becca asked.

"What kind of a question is that? Besides, Linc told me he's going back to Dallas after the first of the year."

"To stay?" Sunny asked.

"I don't know. He has issues here."

"But he and Jack have just partnered up in the horse-breeding business," Sunny said. "Linc told us he wanted to be a true uncle to Tori, not just see her a couple of times a year."

Under the guise of straightening the veil on her straw cowboy hat, Tracy Lynn glanced across the room where Linc was standing in a semicircle with Jack, Storm and Beau. The only furniture in the living room was a couple of leather club chairs facing the wide-screen television that was hidden in the built-in shelves. She could already imagine this room painted in a pale, buttery faux marble to complement the pecan stain on the wood floor.

She would keep the leather chairs, she decided, and dress them up with a couple of sofas, some wing chairs in different fabrics and textures, and a Persian rug to draw the pieces together. The room begged for a touch of elegance, along with the warm and homey.

As though he'd felt her gaze, Linc turned and caught her staring. Flustered, she turned back to her friends, acting as though she had much more important things on her mind besides him.

As if!

"Come on, girls," she said. "Let's go tour this house." Anything to keep her mind off her sexy husband and her suddenly overactive libido.

Chapter Six

After all their guests had left, Linc hauled the trash bags outside. He stopped to breathe deeply of the crisp night air, seasoned with the scent of horses.

He wasn't sorry he'd agreed to start a joint venture here in Hope Valley with his brother. It made good sense for a man to branch out, to create a backup so he'd never find himself pinned in a corner, helpless to defend himself against events or people he had no control over. Jack had faced that very situation not long ago when an infectious cattle disease threatened to wipe out his entire herd.

Everyone needed a cushion of safety, whether it was a nest-egg savings account, a diversified means of income, or merely a home where they were protected, sheltered from angry words and drunken rages.

His gut tightened with the familiar hatred, and Linc slammed the door on his thoughts. Every time he turned around in Hope Valley he was tripping over something that brought back bitter memories of his father. He didn't like the feelings of rage that flared so unexpectedly.

The volatile emotion was the one thing in his life he couldn't claim mastery over.

And it was the one thing that could prevent him from staying here.

How could he spend the rest of his life constantly fighting his phantoms? He needed to be in control of himself and his surroundings—because his childhood had been so *out* of control.

He saw Buck chasing a rabbit but didn't whistle for him. The dog would come in through the pet door when he was ready.

Back in the kitchen, he shut off the lights, then walked back through the house toward the soft music playing on the stereo. Barely two strides into the living room, he came to a jarring halt, nearly tripping over his own booted feet.

''Good God Almighty,'' he breathed. Spellbound, he watched as Tracy Lynn swayed to the rhythm of a country-and-western song, her body flowing in slow, sinuous movements. She appeared utterly lost in the moment, and so incredibly gorgeous he could hardly believe she was right here in his living room, and he was watching her.

Married to her.

Her jeans rode well below her navel, her form-fitting top about an inch above. She'd removed her denim jacket soon after they'd come indoors, causing him a great deal of discomfort the rest of the afternoon. Her stomach was flat, her arms sleek and defined.

She sure didn't look pregnant.

Her straw cowboy hat, no longer sporting the veil, was pulled low on her forehead, casting her face in shadow. Her head was tilted back, her eyes were closed, and her full lips were moist and parted, tempting him to ease on over and slowly lick the sexy arch of her neck.

She was a sensual woman, a woman comfortable in her skin. And watching her dance made his jaw slack and the rest of his body rock hard. A smart man would turn around and head in the opposite direction.

But intelligence didn't stand a prayer against temptation.

He walked across the room. ''Mind if I cut in?''

Her eyes opened slowly, sensuously, as though she'd been expecting him. Leading with her hips, she melted against him, her arms sliding around his neck like the whisper of a silk slip trailing over his skin.

She matched her steps to his as Faith Hill and Tim McGraw sang about wanting to make love.

The brim of her hat brushed his, her blue eyes open, honest and holding his dead on.

His stomach took an elevator-dropping dive, and he was sure his groin passed it on the way up.

Her sultry, graceful moves were innate rather than calculated. She didn't shy away, or act coy, or try to deny that she was responding to him, and to the suggestive lyrics of the song.

And Linc was burning hot.

"I have something for you," she said.

You? he prayed. *Naked in my bed?*

She put a few inches of distance between them and reached into the pocket of her jeans. He didn't know how she could actually *fit* anything besides herself inside those pants.

She brought her hand out and opened her palm.

His heart and stomach changed places.

His ring. The small horseshoe of diamonds sparkled in the overhead light.

"Where did you get that?" His voice was low and raw.

"From the lake where you threw it thirteen years ago."

"You were there?" He couldn't take his eyes off the circle of gold and diamonds.

"Yes. I was going through my 'poet' stage and figured the serenity of water might inspire me to write the next celebrated classic. You didn't seem in the mood for company, so I stayed where I was by the tree at the edge of the Anderleys' place."

"How did you find the ring?" He finally lifted his gaze to meet hers.

"It practically landed at my feet. I hope you didn't have your heart set on capturing the attention of any major league scouts. You're not the greatest pitcher."

He smiled slightly, didn't take offense. Her tone was light, yet there was a vulnerability in her eyes, a watchfulness, a hesitation as though she was embarrassed about whatever thoughts were scrolling through her head.

"After you left the lake, I waded in to see what you'd thrown. I knew there was a shallow area right in front of the cottonwood where I was sitting, and since I'd seen the splash, I was pretty sure that whatever it was had landed on this side of the dropoff."

"That was my grandfather's ring," he said. "My mom gave it to me before my fingers had even grown thick enough to fit the band. She told me the ring was lucky. I chucked it that day because I felt as if I hadn't had any luck at all in my life. Me and my old man were butting heads as usual, and I'd ended up with his bull whip wrapped around my chest."

"Oh, Linc. That image makes me so mad I could catch fire! How could any parent treat their child...?" She stopped, took a breath. "Does the ring bring back bad memories, then?"

He shook his head. "No. Just the opposite." He wasn't used to someone expressing anger on his behalf, championing him. Tracy Lynn's attitude moved him more than he wanted to admit. "I've always regretted my impulsive fit. Gramps was a good man. I looked up to him. I never thought I'd see this ring again."

Instead of luck, what the unique band had truly symbolized to him was love. But that day by the lake, hatred had bred self-pity.

He'd known that staying in this town would destroy him, known that he could never call it home.

Yet here he was, standing in the living room of a

house he'd built on the exact spot his maternal grandfather, Noah Sully, had erected his own homestead years before Linc was even born. Two weeks after Gramps died, Russell Slade had bulldozed the house.

''When you gave me the wedding band today,'' Tracy Lynn said, ''I remembered this one. I don't know why I kept it all these years. Maybe I was saving it for you. I thought you should have it back, that maybe it could even serve as a wedding ring—a pretend one, of course.''

She stretched her hand closer, an indication that he should take the ring.

''Uh-uh.'' He held out his left hand, palm down. ''You put it on me.''

He wasn't sure why he tossed out the challenge. When she took his hand in hers and pushed the ring over his knuckle, he wished he hadn't. Her touch, and the thoughtfulness of saving this ring for him all these years, seemed to take on a much deeper meaning.

The band still fit him, and a sudden memory of himself as a seventeen-year-old boy flashed in his mind. These were the same hands that had touched Tracy Lynn's smooth skin—platonically—when he'd come to her rescue and scattered a group of jocks whose teasing had gotten out of hand.

He also recalled that her daddy had refused to listen to explanations and had made it very clear that Linc wasn't welcome anywhere near his house or his daughter.

''You seem to have a habit of rescuing me,'' she

said as though she'd read his mind, walked with him through the same reminiscence. Her voice was soft, her eyes trained on his hand as she stroked his knuckles with her fingertips, then measured his palm against hers as if surprised that its shape and size hadn't changed in thirteen years.

The CD player changed disks with a sharp click.

When she lifted her gaze to his, he slid his hand around her waist and up the center of her back, pulling her against his chest as he slowly rocked her to the rhythm of the ballad playing now.

He wasn't sure if it was his imagination or wishful thinking, but he could have sworn he felt the hard press of her nipples against his chest.

"What are you feeling?" he asked against her temple.

"Desire," she said honestly. "Like it's my wedding night for real, even though I know it's not. But you know when someone tells you something's off limits and it makes it all the more enticing?"

Her stark honesty constantly caught him off guard. "Mmm."

"I've been thinking about that a lot lately. Wondering. Is that why I'm feeling this way?"

His feet were no longer moving with the music, yet their bodies swayed, rubbing and pressing from hip to chest. He started to suggest her emotions were the result of alcohol, but then recalled that the only drinkers in the small crowd had been the grandmothers.

"Maybe," he said when he was sure his voice

would work. He looked down at her, pressed his hand against the center of her back, stilling her movements. "But I'm feeling it, too."

Her fingers went to his hair, and she lifted his hat off, tossing it behind him onto a chair. He returned the favor and sent hers sailing in the opposite direction.

In a move that felt as natural as breathing, he lowered his head and kissed her. She met him more than halfway, proving once more that her sensuality wasn't merely a facade.

Fire ignited in his gut. He deepened the kiss, forgetting every one of his reservations. She tasted of lemonade and smelled like a bouquet of white orchids. She was as rare as the flower itself.

"I've wanted to do that again since this afternoon," he said against her lips. "And a lot more."

Tracy Lynn wondered if anyone had ever felt as much want as she did now. Life had been a series of emotional ups and downs lately. The agony of trying to get pregnant, the elation when she finally did. Then the terror of possibly losing her father and finding herself in a marriage she'd never in her wildest dreams imagined would take place.

"Would it be so wrong to pretend that this is a real wedding night?" she asked softly. "I can't get pregnant twice, and..." Her voice trailed off. Perhaps she was being too forward, but life was a fragile thing, and dreams could disappear as quickly as a sudden heart attack or incurable disease.

She wasn't a young, innocent girl. "There's a

unique chemistry between us,'' she whispered. ''I don't understand it. I just...*need.*''

''Are you sure?''

She closed her eyes. ''Don't make me beg, Linc.''

Before the words were hardly uttered, he swept her into his arms and carried her up the stairs, still kissing her as he pushed through the doorway of his bedroom.

He toed off his boots, laid her on the bed and followed her down, fitting his body over hers. For what seemed like hours, he simply kissed her, kept his hands cupping her face as though they had the rest of their lives to do just this. Holding his weight on his elbows, he showered her with kisses so tender she thought she might weep, then slowly turned up the heat with kisses that inflamed.

When he came up for air, she saw a hint of reluctance mingled with the hot passion in his eyes. She understood, felt the same emotions...and so much more.

But she didn't want either of them to entertain second thoughts. Something had happened between them at that wedding ceremony today, something good and decent and right.

And if tonight was all she could have of him, so be it. No one could predict what tomorrow would bring...or take away.

She didn't need his nobility just now.

She needed his touch.

Reaching between them, she began unbuttoning his shirt. His stomach sucked in as the backs of her fingers brushed his skin from neck to belt buckle. Sliding her hands inside his shirt, she reveled in the hard muscles rippling beneath her palms.

She was about to push the material off his shoulders when he stopped her. Capturing her hands, he kissed her knuckles, then removed the shirt himself.

"My turn," he said, his voice barely audible.

He started with her boots and socks, then her jeans, stroking and massaging every inch of skin he uncovered. Taking his time. His touch was featherlight, yet his fingertips exerted just the right amount of pressure to make her writhe as he skimmed them up the inside of her thighs. Driving her mad.

She had never been undressed with such exquisitely erotic care.

When his hands bracketed her hips, his thumbs lightly stroking over the silk of her panties, Tracy Lynn whimpered. The sound astounded her. She couldn't recall a single time a man had made her *whimper.* Not that she'd had all that many lovers, but for a very long time she *had* been actively searching for a white knight to father her babies.

And now…her breath stalled as his hands slid up her rib cage, lifting her shirt. The elastic of the built-in bra pulled against the bottom of her breasts, then tugged free as he skimmed the top over her head.

For a long moment he sat back on his heels, caressing her with only his hungry gaze. A slight chill pervaded the sparsely furnished room, and her skin pebbled with goose flesh, her nipples contracting from both the cool air and hot desire.

And still, he just stared, as though truly, utterly mesmerized. Either that, or he was about to change his mind and back out.

"Linc?"

"You are so beautiful." He traced the outer contours of her breasts, coming so close but never touching the aching centers. "So soft. So perfect."

The utter reverence in his tone aroused her beyond reason. She tugged him down to her, needing to feel him, skin to skin.

His mouth covered hers, the expertise he brought to the kiss shooting her into a maelstrom of desire so fierce she could hardly remember her own name. She arched her hips against his, needing the pressure, something, anything to put out the fire running rampant through her body.

"Take off your pants," she urged against his lips even as her hands were sliding between their bodies, fumbling with the snap at his waist.

"Babe." He intercepted her hand, rested his forehead against hers, his breathing as strained as hers was. "It's been a while for me, and I'm about to go over the edge just looking at you."

She went utterly still. He had the kind of bad-boy sex appeal that should have women waiting in line to claim him. His admission that he hadn't been with a woman in a while thrilled her, made her feel special. Even more so because she was the one wearing his ring, lying beneath him in his bed.

Even if it wasn't for the long haul.

"Well, it's been three years for me," she said, "so

if it's a race you're looking for to see who'll lose control first, don't bet on yourself."

His mouth kicked up at the corners. "Three years? You been playing hard to get, Miss Prom Queen?"

"That's *Ms.* if you don't mind."

Linc stood, unbuckled his belt and removed his jeans and boxers, then knelt on the mattress and slid her panties down her legs, tossing them on the floor. He kissed the mound of her femininity, her navel, her breasts, licked his way up her neck and jaw, tasted her perfume.

He pressed his lips to her eyelids, her temple, the corner of her mouth, wanting to rush, *needing* to rush, yet taking his time. Hovering a breath away from her lips, he murmured, "Mrs."

He didn't give her an opportunity to respond. With lips and hands he mapped her body, gauging her desire, watching, aching, enjoying, taking her up to a fever pitch, then gently easing her down.

He loved the little moans she uttered, the way her body responded to his slightest touch. She reached for him, but he evaded. He wasn't finished with her. Not by a long shot.

"I've waited a lifetime for you, Tracy Lynn. Indulge me, okay?" He wondered what she would do if he told her that he'd watched her from afar ever since he was just a boy. That he'd yearned.

Would she think he was a sap if he admitted that she'd always been his dream girl? That every year she was the wish he'd made on his birthday candle?

That hers was the name he whispered when loneliness closed in?

Knowing the words would only complicate the temporary situation they'd been thrust into, he let his hands and lips speak for him, groaning when he felt her restless surrender.

"Linc..." Impatience hummed over her heated skin, thickened her voice, her hands fisting the sheets.

"Uh-uh. I'm thinking this is going to take all night." He wanted to call the shots, wanted to make sure that any thoughts or experiences she'd had with other men were wiped from her mind. Replaced by only him.

This urgent need was new to him. In the past when he'd taken a woman to bed, he'd only been interested in the satisfaction of release. Mutual gratification with no strings.

But Tracy Lynn was different. With her, he *wanted* strings.

"I'll be dead before morning," she complained. He felt her tense, knew that reality had intruded, that she'd just reminded herself of her father's uncertain fate.

"I promise to revive you." His mouth closed over the peak of her breast.

Tracy Lynn usually obeyed rules, but not this time. She wanted to return the pleasure, participate, touch him as he was touching her.

She gripped the back of his neck, pressed him more firmly against her aching flesh, arched her back as sensations held her in the grip of the most intense pleasure she'd ever experienced. She felt drugged, her limbs heavy and weak with desire.

His hair slid through her fingers as he moved down her body, his tongue tracing a path down the center of her stomach.

A distant part of her mind realized his intention. She thought to stop him, yet within seconds, with his mouth, he brought her to a climax so explosively exquisite she nearly fainted. Giving her no respite, his fingers replaced his lips, prolonging the spasms, intensifying the orgasm.

She screamed, writhed and pleaded. If she could have formulated a coherent thought, she might have told him she really wasn't kidding about that dying remark. Surely there was a limit to the amount of pleasure a woman could endure.

Oh, but what a way to go. Her heels dug into the mattress, her breath coming out in whimpering pants.

"Yes," he murmured. "That's the way, babe. Once more." He moved between her legs, entered her in one smooth, powerful thrust.

Scooping his arm beneath her hips, he lifted her, held her steady as he pressed into her. Feminine muscles squeezed him, pulsing hot and slick around him. Sweat beaded at his temple, prickled over his spine.

He ground his back teeth, felt his release building as her body milked him, prayed he could maintain control. She was so sensitized, he knew she needed a minute to settle before he took her over the next soaring hurdle.

But she snatched the reins right out of his hands. Wrapping her legs around him, she rotated her hips in a way that drove him wild.

"Now!" she panted. "Right now, Linc!"

He thrust into her, hard and deep, faster and faster, until she cried out, her fingernails digging into his back, her legs gripping him.

Release slammed though him with the force of a charging stallion, uncivilized, powerful, the sensations so stunning and intense he thought he'd shatter.

And in that moment he knew he'd made a big mistake by turning his lifelong fantasy into reality.

Because now he would never stop wanting her.

Chapter Seven

Tracy Lynn wanted to know who let the darn cricket into the house. She wasn't a morning person, and the incessant chirping was driving her batty. She burrowed deeper into the pillow, trying to shut out the noise and drift back to sleep. The sound changed to an insistent beep, and she groaned.

Alarm clock. Suelinda must have accidentally changed the setting while dusting.

Eyes still closed, she reached over to slap the snooze button, but her hand merely whooshed through vacant air. Seriously annoyed that she was forced to wake up before she was ready, she opened her eyes. Frowned.

Memory pushed through the fog of sleep and she shot straight up in the bed. Linc's bed.

Two things registered at once. She was stark naked. And she was alone.

Looking around wildly for the stupid clock, she found it on the floor, made a dive for it and managed to get it turned off. The electronic numbers read

5:30 a.m. Good grief. The chickens weren't even up this early!

Her heart thudded in her chest as she flopped back onto the pillows and pulled the covers to her chin, the events of the previous night at last registering in her brain. She felt the heat of a blush steal over her skin from the tips of her toes to the top of her head.

Mercy. Never in her life had she experienced anything like Linc's brand of lovemaking.

Where was he now? She hadn't anticipated ending up in bed with him the very first night, and now she was suffering some morning-after jitters, unsure of the ground rules, unsure of where she stood.

She dragged the sheet off the bed and got up, heading toward the arched opening that led to the master bathroom. When she'd toured the house yesterday with Becca, Sunny and Donetta, this bathroom had literally taken her breath away. It mimicked the size of the master suite and housed the most awesome shower she'd ever seen. Completely enclosed floor to ceiling with a solid wall of thick glass on one side, polished stone on the other three and a skylight above, it could easily hold a king-size bed.

She dropped the sheet to the floor and turned on the water. Heat lamps, camouflaged in the stone, chased away the morning chill. With multiple shower heads cascading water from the stone walls, it was like walking into a private grotto.

And it was a crying shame to be all alone in such an extravagantly romantic surrounding.

She finished her shower, wrapped herself in a lusciously thick towel, then crossed the hall to the guest room to unpack and dress.

By the time she set out in search of Linc, the sun was just beginning to light the sky. Her breath clouded on the early-morning air, and she pulled her coat closer as she stepped off the back porch and headed toward the elaborate outbuildings.

Sounds seemed sharper at this time of the day when the world was just coming awake—the coo of a dove, the whistle of a bobwhite, the whinny and nicker of horses. Mist, permeated with the scent of animals, hovered over the ground.

The plank fences cordoning paddocks, corrals and property borders were painted a nutmeg hue rather than the traditional white. Several men were already out exercising horses.

She found Linc in the horse barn, his coat off, the sleeves of his shirt rolled up as he forked hay into an empty stall and spread it around. For a moment, she stood in awe—of the man and of the facilities.

His house was at least six thousand square feet. This barn was twice that size.

Tethered outside the stall that Linc was feverishly raking was a beautiful chestnut horse. Tracy Lynn didn't know squat about Thoroughbreds, but this one seemed exceptionally well formed, reminding her of the sleekly toned body of an athlete.

The horse lifted its proud head and made a sound as though clearing its throat. A chicken streaked across the center aisle of the barn and dove beneath one of the stall doors like a woman who'd been caught half naked when the preacher came to call.

Both occurrences startled her. She must have made a noise, because Linc straightened and looked at her, leaning his weight on the pitchfork.

''Hi,'' she said, feeling a little awkward. She wasn't quite sure how to act after last night.

He dipped his head in a nod, the brim of his hat partially concealing his expression.

Okay. Not the most demonstrative greeting, perhaps, but cordial enough. She started toward him, but the horse swung its head around and she halted, deciding not to go any nearer.

''You here to help muck out stalls?'' Linc finally asked.

''Is that what you're doing?'' She shoved her hands in her pockets. ''Your horse doesn't look like he wants me to join you.''

''She,'' he corrected. ''Her name's Pride of Priscilla—Prissy for short. She's a sweetheart. Just don't walk behind her and startle her.''

A subtle change came over him when he talked about the mare. His face lost the guarded tension that was usually there. *Horses are easy,* he'd said. Even if he hadn't made that remark, she would have pegged him as a man more comfortable around animals than people.

She moved forward once again and cautiously reached up to rub Prissy's nose. The horse jerked her head and Tracy Lynn snatched away her hand, quickly stepping back. Prissy did the same, yanking at her tether rope.

"Whoa," Linc said. Abandoning his pitchfork, he was outside the stall in less than a second, his gloved hands gently stroking Prissy's neck, urging her head back down. "Easy, girl. You're okay." Neither his voice nor his movements would have stirred the hair on a fluffy rabbit. "Haven't been around horses much, hmm?"

"Not a lot, no." Her knees felt like spaghetti. She wondered if Prissy could sense that.

"I'd have thought the gal who was a cheerleader, prom queen and Miss Hope Valley would have surely taken riding lessons and entered fancy competitions."

She frowned at his tone. It sounded almost mocking. What had happened to the tender, loving man who'd shown her bliss last night? This morning, he was acting as though they were barely acquainted.

"When I was a child, one of Daddy's horses got spooked and broke my collarbone when she pinned me against the wall of the barn. Since then, I've been a little leery. I know it seems irrational, but even now that I've grown considerably, their size is magnified in my mind. It's as though I'm seeing this horse through a little girl's eyes and height—and I'm a bit intimidated."

Linc swore softly and ducked under Prissy's neck, putting himself between her and the horse. "Childhood trauma is tough to get over on your own. You seem to want to, though, am I right?"

"Yes. They're beautiful animals, and I feel foolish."

He tugged off his leather glove and held out his hand toward her. "Come on. I won't let her step on you. Trust me."

She took his hand.

"Stroke her neck. Let her see you."

With Linc standing next to her, she was able to indulge her fascination. She'd always had the urge to put her arms around a horse, lay her cheek against its neck and hug, much the same as she'd do with a dog.

And that was exactly what she did now. Although her heartbeat drummed in her ears, she laughed delightedly.

"She's so soft and warm. I could just cuddle right up to her."

Prissy seemed to agree and bobbed her head, bumping against the top of Tracy Lynn's head.

"She's not eating my hair, is she?"

"Not much. You should still have enough left to fix in a ponytail."

Tracy Lynn pulled back and grinned at him. "I never knew you were such a clown."

He didn't return her smile, just stared at her, and she started to get a bad feeling.

"We need to talk about last night," he said.

Okay. She wasn't real crazy about his tone, either. He didn't have to elaborate. She could tell by the look on his face that he regretted sleeping with her.

Hurt and embarrassment stung her insides, but she

would drink out of a slimy horse trough before she'd let him know that. She gave Prissy's cheek another soft scratch, then stepped back.

"It was no big deal, Linc. Let's not turn it into one. We're two consenting adults who acted on a perfectly natural need. Nothing's changed."

"Do you honestly believe that?"

"Does it really matter?" she countered. "We made a deal."

"Sex wasn't part of the deal."

"Well, we can't very well take it back, now can we? What do you want from me? My word of honor that I won't try to entice you back into bed? Fine. You've got it. God, this is embarrassing." She whirled around. "I'm going to the hospital."

"Babe." He caught her arm. "I'm only thinking about you."

"I'm a big girl, Linc. I can think for myself."

"I just don't want you to get hurt. You're too trusting."

"Oh, for crying out loud. Did you *plan* to hurt me?"

He let go of her arm. "Not intentionally."

The flash of anguish in his eyes and his tone dissolved her irritation in an instant. She knew enough about his past to understand his inner wounds—after all, her best friend was married to his brother. Last night she'd felt his outer wounds—the scars on his back—and had nearly wept. She hadn't asked about them because making love wasn't the time to resurrect bad memories.

''I understood what you were telling me the other day when you said you'd be leaving after the first of the year. I wish I could erase all the old ghosts for you, but that's something you have to do on your own. I went into this with my eyes open, Linc. Neither one of us made promises, so unintentionally hurting each other shouldn't be a concern. I won't cling if you decide to go back to Dallas.''

With that, she turned to leave. Honor had prompted him to marry her when he'd clearly had one foot out the door, and now he was trapped, forced to subject himself to reminders he shouldn't have to deal with on a daily basis.

''Trace?'' At the sound of his voice, she paused. ''Let me know if they move up the surgery schedule, and I'll come sit with you.''

She started to object, then just nodded.

That was what a real husband would do.

TRACY SPENT THE NEXT TWO DAYS at the hospital. It wasn't easy dodging her father's questions, and she felt as though she was simply digging herself into a deeper pit of lies.

''Everything going okay between you and Linc?'' he asked.

''Yes. Just fine.'' If you considered being ignored *fine*.

''Can't help but notice he hasn't been around.''

''He has work to do, Daddy.'' In that respect, Linc and her father were very much alike. Both were workaholics.

''You said you renewed your acquaintance with Linc when you went to Dallas?''

''Mmm. Would you like some water?'' She picked up the plastic pitcher, remembered it was empty. ''Sorry. I forgot they starve you before surgery. It's a good thing you already had the IV in. Dehydration makes it difficult to find a vein.'' She tidied the hospital tray, shifted the box of tissues and aligned it with his reading glasses—for the third time in as many minutes.

''I remember how they used to poke Mama's arms, trying to find a vein that wasn't collapsed. She was such a trooper through it....'' Her mouth snapped shut as her father put his hand over hers.

Oh, God. What was she thinking? He was about to have major surgery and she was babbling on about Mama—who'd died in this very hospital.

What if *he* died? What if he died still believing the lie between them?

''Come on, sweet pea. Don't go diggin' up the graveyard and borrowing trouble.''

She laughed, embarrassed that the sound was partly a sob. ''Linc always says that to me—that I'm borrowing trouble.''

''That's because you do.'' She jumped at the sound of Linc's voice. He placed his hands on her shoulders from behind.

''Darn it, Linc. You scared me half to death.'' The last word was out with no hope of recall when she realized its inappropriateness.

Linc grinned and reached past her to shake hands

with her father. "Your daughter is a real worrier," he said.

This moment of male bonding was all well and good, Tracy Lynn thought. But she didn't appreciate being the subject.

Oh, who was she kidding? She was touched beyond words that Linc had remembered the surgery. That he'd come. For her. She hadn't thought he would, despite the fact that she'd told him the date and time as he'd requested.

Since their "morning after" in the barn, she'd slept in the guest room. They'd hardly crossed paths, and she didn't need a written memo to figure out the avoidance was deliberate. Yes, she'd been at the hospital a good many hours over the past two days, but not *all* of them.

The passionate lovemaking of their wedding night might never have happened.

The man had a noble streak as wide as Texas, and a misguided notion that she needed protection from herself—evidently so she wouldn't get her feelings all tangled and start setting up housekeeping for real.

Of course, he was too late for that. Her feelings had been engaged even *before* they'd made love. And neither avoidance nor a divorce would change that, so it was flat-out silly that they couldn't just act like two normal adults living under the same roof.

"Maybe you ought to come on over here and slip your arm in this boa constrictor machine, sweet pea. Make sure you're not overrevving your blood pressure with all that excess worrying."

"My blood pressure's fine, thanks, Daddy."

"We could hook you up to these alien skin suckers." He plucked one of the wires taped to his chest. "Feed your heart information out to Ellie's monitor at the nurses' station."

Linc chuckled.

"Cute," Tracy Lynn drawled. "What got you so perked up all of a sudden?"

"Censorship gets my juices flowing. Might even have to make that part of my campaign. Now, let's see here." Jerald drummed his fingers on the bedsheet. "We've covered the graveyard. Runnin' into trouble with veins and needles. Dehydration. Dying. What else aren't we supposed to talk about in a hospital room?"

"Blood's probably not a good idea," Linc said helpfully, his expression once again bland.

Tracy Lynn bumped him with her shoulder. "Cut it out, funny guy— Oh, damn." A bubble of laughter escaped her throat, and she pressed a palm to her forehead. "This is morbid. And sick. And you're both idiots." Nerves boiled in her empty stomach. "I'm going to do something productive, like pace."

Deliberately ignoring them, she strode to the window, hugging her arms around her ribs as she looked out over the hospital's manicured landscape scattered with oaks and a naked magnolia tree.

"I don't imagine major bypass surgery is going to be any picnic," Linc said. She could see his reflection in the window as he sat down in the chair beside her father's bed. "You ready for it?"

"Ready as I'll ever be. I've been wondering what kind of power tools those old boys use in the operating room to saw open a rib cage."

"Probably just a plain ol' circular saw. Let's hope your doctor has a steady hand."

Tracy Lynn's jaw dropped.

"You can bet I'm going to check him out before they gas me," Jerald said.

She turned, leaned against the windowsill and watched the two men in her life converse as though there'd never been an unspoken social line drawn between them.

Her head wasn't so far in the clouds that she didn't recognize the intangible thread of tension between her father and Linc. There had to be unresolved history eating at both of them. Even though her father had given every indication he would have resorted to a true shotgun wedding if pushed, she had no idea how he truly felt about Linc as a son-in-law.

And how could Linc, after being on the receiving end of her father's scorn during his youth, sit here so casually and joke with the man who'd at one time judged him and found him lacking?

I've got a bank account that ensures no one closes a door on me.

That one statement said a lot.

He was a grown man now, well respected and enormously successful. Yet he still carried deep wounds.

Linc glanced over and caught her staring. The heat of a blush bloomed on her cheeks. She fought the urge to duck her head, to pretend that she *hadn't* been looking, that her eyes had just happened to skim in his direction at the same time he chose to look her way. An accident, nothing more.

But the way his eyes had softened just now as he'd gazed at her…

Oh, for pity's sake. Impatiently she pushed away from the windowsill and resumed pacing.

My gosh, she was losing it. Big time. Just because he'd saved her father's life, laid false claim to the child in her womb, then rocked the very foundation of her world by making love to her with an earth-shattering intensity guaranteed to ruin her for any other man, there was no call to be assigning fanciful meanings to this tough guy's expressions.

Tough guy. An apt description. But he was also gentle. And in the midst of mind-numbing fear over her father's health, there shouldn't be a single, valid reason she was reacting to Lincoln Slade as though someone had doused them in irresistible pheromones.

Other than the fact that they were now married.

"Seems to me," Linc said to Jerald, "they could just run you through a table saw and get a much more precise cut than wrestling with a handheld power tool."

"Boy, that'd gut me like a catfish. They'd have to saw one end of me clean in two to get to where they're going, and both those ends of me have a will-ful head that'd strenuously object."

Linc grinned, leaned back in the chair with his ankle resting on the opposite knee. "You wouldn't have to give up the family jewels. The doc could rig up something similar to those light fixtures dentists use. Just swing the arm down, let her rip, and there you go.''

Tracy Lynn shuddered at their morbid humor.

Ellie approached them, holding a chart. ''Time to take a ride. How is everyone this morning?'' she asked. ''Bright-eyed and bushy-tailed, I hope?''

''My eyes and tail are feeling a little pea green after listening to these two re-create the chain-saw massacre,'' Tracy Lynn complained.

Linc stood and moved next to her, his gray-blue eyes searching hers. ''Are you feeling sick?'' he asked quietly, his gaze dipping almost imperceptibly to her stomach.

She wanted to lay her cheek against his chest and hug him for remembering. For caring. ''Not that kind of sick,'' she answered just as quietly.

They stepped back as Ellie and a male nurse hooked the IV pole to the hospital bed, laid her father's health chart next to him, then released the brake on the rolling bed and wheeled him out of the CCU toward the elevators.

Tracy Lynn walked beside him and held his hand. ''Can we all fit in the elevator?'' she asked.

''Sure,'' Ellie said as they filed through the steel doors and crowded around the bed. ''Linc, would you push the first-floor button, please?''

The nurse turned back to Tracy Lynn. ''Y'all can wait in the main lobby. I'll let Dr. Bruley know you're there, and he'll come out and talk to you when he's finished with your dad's surgery. Most of the time he makes it to the patient's room to discuss any concerns the family has beforehand, but he's running a bit behind schedule this morn—"

"In case anybody cares," Jerald interrupted, "while they're talking about me as if I'm not here, I happen to be wide awake—or bright-eyed, I believe was the term. And last time I checked I had a sound mind and excellent hearing."

Ellie patted his shoulder. "Of course you do, handsome."

"Although I can't claim that certain parts of me are quite so bushy anymore," he grumbled, shifting his head back to frown at the nurse. "Some blond-haired maniac took a razor to my chest and shaved it bald."

"And I dulled two razors in the process," Ellie said with a grin.

"Chin up, Daddy. We'll just tell everyone you're in training for the Olympic swim team." The elevator dinged its arrival at the first floor. Linc held the doors open while they exited in reverse order.

"That would require a *whole* lot more shaving," Ellie quipped as she pushed the gurney through the hallway.

"Just because a man's buck naked under these pneumonia gowns, that's no excuse to be taking unfair advantage and broadcasting his secrets."

"I was talking about your legs, Mayor. Whatever are you referring to?"

Tracy Lynn laughed at Ellie's false Southern innocence, and Linc exchanged a look of male commiseration with Jerald.

''I hope you all know I have orders to keep my blood pressure down. And—''

''Mayor Randolph!'' Betty Jo Gridelle, one of the clerks at the post office, rushed over. ''Why, I thought that was you. I'm just here to pay a call on Connie Nance. She slipped in the tub and wrenched her back. Nasty business. You know how those back injuries can just pain you something fierce. Dru Taggat over at the seniors' center has got herself all het up thinking Connie's going to claim she hurt herself in aerobics class and sue. I keep telling Dru that's not going to happen. I was lucky enough to stop by at the right moment—and there was Connie, naked as the day she was born. Thankfully, I got her covered up all proper before the fireman got there—''

''You give Miz Nance our best,'' Linc interrupted smoothly, patting Betty Jo on the shoulder. ''And be sure and tell her the mayor said 'hey.'''

''Oh, she'll be thrilled. Good luck, Mayor Randolph.''

Jerald gave a stiff nod and briefly lifted the hand not attached to the IV. ''Damn it,'' he muttered. ''Is it necessary to parade me through the common areas for all and sundry to gawk at?''

''But, Daddy, you look so *fine* in your blue paper hat.''

''Your mother spoiled you entirely too much,'' he said to Tracy Lynn, then looked at Linc. ''Much obliged for running interference.''

"End of the line, kids," Ellie said, hitting the button on the wall for the automatic doors.

Tracy Lynn leaned over and kissed her father. "I love you, Daddy. We'll see you in a little while."

She felt Linc's hands cup her shoulders and she leaned back against his chest, watching until the electronic doors closed off her view.

"He'll be fine," Linc said.

"I'm not sure it was right that we were all joking around when this is so serious."

"Babe. Who wants a bunch of anxious handwringers hovering to remind a patient what he's facing? Best thing is to keep his mind off his health fears. Why do you think Ellie flirts the way she does?"

"You're right." She fell into step with him when he guided her toward the waiting room.

"Where are your Sweetheart pals?" he asked.

"I didn't tell them what time the surgery was scheduled."

"Why not?"

She shrugged and sank down on an overstuffed, cactus-green love seat that faced the elevators so she'd spot the doctor when he came out. She didn't want a re-creation of the day her mother had died, when practically everyone she knew and loved had camped out in the waiting room. She knew it was irrational, but she thought that if she treated her daddy's surgery as no big deal, didn't have to look at a bunch of worried faces that reflected her own fears, everything would turn out fine. "It'll just be easier to call everyone when the surgery's over."

Linc sat next to her. "The girls are not going to be happy with you."

"They'll be okay." Although she didn't want a crowd, she was glad that Linc was here. Her dad had actually perked up when Linc had brought up the difficulty of the surgery, not shying away from the seriousness as Tracy Lynn had been trying to do. Even Ellie's teasing had brought a spark of color to her father's face.

"I'm not so sure all of Ellie's flirting is strictly in the line of duty."

"Maybe not," he agreed. "Does that bother you?"

"No. Mama's been gone for ten years. I'm kind of surprised Daddy hasn't dated anyone."

"Could be because he has you to take care of him. He doesn't need anyone else."

She frowned. "I don't take care of him. I mean, I organize parties and act as hostess, things like that."

"But you still live with him."

The statement sounded more like an accusation. "Not anymore. Did you forget so soon?" She was acutely aware of his thigh pressed against hers, but she wasn't going to be the first one to move.

"I didn't forget. Do you want me to rephrase?"

Something in his tone rubbed her the wrong way. "Oh, I think I can keep up," she drawled sweetly. "There *are* actually a few brain cells under this blond hair." She scooted to the edge of the sofa cushion, twisted to look at him. ''This is the second time you've brought up this subject. Why does it bug you so much that I live at home?''

''*Did* live. And it's none of my business, but since you asked, I think your father takes advantage of you.''

''He does not! Where would you get a lame idea like that?''

''From the way he treated you on the courthouse steps, for one. And from the way he guilted you into getting married, for another.''

Defensive, conscious that they weren't the only people in the waiting room, she kept her voice at a peeved whisper. ''Correct me if I'm wrong, but I could have sworn it was *you* who kicked over the hornet's nest in the 'whose baby is this?' fiasco. And I seem to recall that it was *you* who lobbied so aggressively in favor of my father's demands.''

''If you'll stop a minute and think back, in both those cases I did what was best for the situation. Someone had to make a decision and act. I might have been a little fast out of the gate in regards to the baby announcement, but I rectified that with the marriage. I don't know why you're still climbing all over *me* about this. It was your father who acted as though he was ashamed.''

''I can't believe you're attacking my father when he's on an operating table and could die. And at least he was honest about his feelings and didn't hide out in the barn like *some* people I know.'' She shot up off the couch and walked away, not sure where she was going.

She hadn't meant to blurt out that last part.

Arguing with Linc was like butting her head against a brick wall. Her emotions were so close to the surface she thought she'd explode. And creeping around like strangers in his cavernous house only increased her edginess.

She wasn't sure where her strength had gone, but she was having a great deal of trouble finding the stuffing that usually kept her together.

Maybe some of what Linc said was true. She'd had similar thoughts over the years, bouts of resentment over some of her father's demands, but she'd buried her resentment in denial, told herself there was nothing wrong with respecting a parent, wanting to please him.

Good Lord, she'd even thought about leaving town so her pregnancy wouldn't embarrass her father.

Needing to get away from Linc, but afraid to wander too far in case she missed the doctor, she walked out of the waiting room and found a private alcove near the elevators. She sat on the floor, her back to the wall, and rested her forehead on her bent knees.

She didn't bother to look up when she felt the warmth of a body easing down next to her. She knew it was Linc. She recognized his scent, the hint of sandalwood and musk that lingered from his aftershave.

He bumped her leg with his, reminding her of grade school, when boys and girls gave each other a light shove or punch on the arm to show affection or to make up.

"Why are we fighting?" she asked, her voice muffled against her knees. "I can't even remember the point."

"The point is, I'm an ass, and my sense of timing sucks."

She lifted her head. "Don't wait for me to contradict you. I've got no argument with that statement."

He shook his head. "You never skirt an issue, do you? You're so open and honest, you just tell it like it is."

"Except when I'm with my father."

"That was my lie, not yours."

She'd never thought much about the aspect of her personality Linc was referring to—her tendency to say what was on her mind. She just expected people to accept her as she was, and had found it was a lot easier to be honest, to let people know exactly where she stood.

With Linc, that wasn't wholly the case. She was holding something back. A very big something.

Because despite the fact that he made her mad enough to spit nails, despite the fact that their lives had traveled such different paths, deep in her bones she believed he was her soul mate.

Chapter Eight

The lights were on in the barn when Tracy Lynn got back to Linc's house. After the doctor had emerged from the operating room to report that the surgery was a success, Linc returned to the ranch, but Tracy Lynn had stayed the rest of the day, doing the very thing her father hated—hovering and watching him sleep.

Truthfully, she felt as though she'd been squeezed through an old-fashioned wringer, then dumped on the floor in a heap. She ought to go straight to bed, but she was too keyed up to settle down.

She put away the food she'd brought home, then found a pad of paper and a measuring tape, and began to sketch out the size and shape of the great room. It was a huge area, combining the kitchen, informal dining and family room, with vaulted ceilings and tall windows that created an illusion of bringing the outdoors inside. She could visualize a blend of antiques and traditional furniture—neutral colors, she decided, accented with subtle shades of red.

The back door opened just as she was checking the distance from the ceiling to the top of the window.

"Babe." Linc scowled and crossed the room, with Buck trailing behind. "You shouldn't be climbing on step stools." She barely had a chance to note the inch mark on the tape before he reached for her.

Her heart danced in her chest, both from being unceremoniously plucked off her perch and from the feel of Linc's hands lingering at her waist. He was all cowboy, from his hat to his boots, and just looking at him robbed her of speech, made her feel like a young girl with a major crush on a pop star.

He stepped back. "What are you doing?"

"Um, I *was* measuring for furniture and drapes."

"That can wait. You've got enough on your plate."

"Well, *you* have very few plates, and even less furniture."

"I've got chairs, a table and a bed. That'll do for now. How's your dad?"

Spoken like a man, she thought. She reached down and scratched Buck's ears. "In pain. Groggy. Probably won't even remember I was there. But the doctor says he's doing okay."

Linc shoved his hands in his pockets. "Did Sunny make it to the hospital?"

"Yes, and so did Donetta and Becca Sue...*before* I had a chance to call them."

He shrugged. "So, I saved you a phone call—or three."

She smiled. ''Thank you. And you were right, they weren't happy that I hadn't asked them to wait through the surgery with me. I just couldn't, though. I know it sounds stupid, but I was scared it would be like Mama all over again—that having a crowd gathered might jinx the procedure.''

''Guess it's a good thing I wasn't around back then. You might have had some trouble tossing me out today. You must be beat.''

It took a moment for her to switch from the image of him not budging from the hospital to his comment about her energy level. ''Actually, I'm wired and I haven't had a drop of coffee. Here.'' She held out the end of the tape measure. ''Make yourself useful and hold this.''

''You're not getting back up on that stool.''

She rolled her eyes. ''And you called *me* a worrier?'' She walked toward the archway, the tape reeling out as Linc held it steady. ''Okay. You can let go now.'' When the tape recoiled, Buck thought this was the start of a new game and gave chase until Linc called him back.

''I don't suppose you have a copy of the blueprints, do you?'' she asked.

''In the study. Did you eat?''

Couldn't the guy stay on track here? ''It would be helpful if I could look at them.''

''I'll get them later. Did you eat?'' he repeated, glancing at her stomach.

Bossy man. Although she had an idea he was thinking about the baby. ''Not yet. I stopped by

Anna's Café and picked up some gumbo and turkey sandwiches. They're in the fridge. All I have to do is heat up the soup—that is, if you don't mind sharing a meal with me.'' He still had that standoffish air about him. One way or another, they were going to have to get past that.

''Have you made an appointment with the doctor yet?''

Honestly! Trying to keep up was making her dizzy. ''I haven't had time. With Daddy in the hospital and everything else…''

''You can spare an hour, babe.''

''Linc, I'm fine. I called Lily O'Rourke and she said there's no problem with me waiting a month—especially since I took the home test so early. Donetta gave me a bottle of the prenatal vitamins Lily prescribed for her, so unless I'm having any problems—which I'm not—there's no rush. All she'd be doing, anyway, is confirming the pregnancy and establishing a due date, but I already know those things.''

He nodded. ''I'll go wash up.''

Tracy Lynn breathed a little easier once Linc went upstairs. He was concerned about her enticing him, yet *he* was the one staring at her with hungry eyes. And it wasn't a craving for Anna's gumbo.

She recorded a few more measurements, then laid the notes on the granite surface of the breakfast bar. Before she commandeered Becca to help her shop, she needed to know more about Linc's personality.

Right now, she knew only the basics. He was a

rich man, yet he wasn't pretentious, so comfort would be foremost. He was tough, but he had a soft side, which meant she could get away with adding a few feminine touches mixed in with some sturdy, masculine pieces.

It was mainly the accents she wanted to personalize, things that were uniquely Linc. She intended to make his house a home, a place of joy and refuge, things he probably hadn't had for a good part of his life.

She tried to tell herself she was motivated by compassion, but honesty had her admitting that her reasons were also selfish.

She wanted this house to feed his soul, heal it. She wanted him to love it so much that he'd stay.

By the time Linc came back downstairs, she'd filled Buck's dish with dry dog food, heated the soup and was arranging the sandwiches on plates.

"You don't have to cook for me," he said.

"I didn't. Anna did. Sit down before the soup gets cold." She put the food on the table and poured lemonade into glasses. "Who usually fixes your meals?"

"I do."

"You cook?"

"Yes. And I'm good at it. Since I've been back, though, Cora and Beau have been leaving little food gifts in my refrigerator, so I haven't really initiated my kitchen."

Tracy Lynn's mind conjured up an image of an entirely different type of initiation. She took a spoonful of soup and burned her mouth, quickly dousing the heat with a gulp of lemonade.

"You okay?" he asked.

"Fine. So, tell me about your hobbies—other than cooking." *And I'll get my mind off of sex.*

"Why?"

"Honestly, are you always so suspicious of people's motives?"

"Habit."

"I'd like to get a feel for what you like to do. What kind of style you have in mind for furniture. I don't want to park a gleaming Steinway in your living room if you hate piano music."

"I like piano music. I don't much go for dinky furniture that looks like it'll break if you sit on it, though."

"I've got you covered there." That, too, she'd known about him. At six-foot-four, he wouldn't appreciate a prissy eighteenth-century chair to relax in at the end of the day. "So, what do you do in your spare time?"

"I don't have a lot of that."

"This is going to be like teaching a mermaid to do the splits," she muttered. "Do you read?"

"Some."

Exasperated, she glared at him. "Like *what?*"

"Westerns, suspense, any books or periodicals on horses—breeding, training, racing."

"Okay, what else?"

"You're not going to give up, are you?"

"No. The more I know about you, the easier it'll

be for me to make buying decisions when you're not around to give your approval.''

''I told you I trust your judgment.''

''Linc...'' She put as much warning into her tone as she could muster.

He let out a breath and leaned back in his chair. ''I play the guitar some. Fly my Cessna every chance I get. Carve things out of wood. I made a chess set for my farrier—the guy who shoes my horses.''

''So you like chess?''

''I like to *look* at a chessboard, but I don't particularly like to play.''

''What else do you carve?''

''Dolls.''

She blinked. ''Dolls?''

His gaze never wavered. ''You heard me.''

There was absolutely no question about his masculinity, and the fact that he stated the hobby without a qualm made her heart melt. She remembered Tori peopling her dollhouse with tiny wooden figurines, recalled being enchanted and impressed. She glanced at his large hands.

''The little miniatures Tori has. You made those, didn't you.''

He nodded. Before today she never would have guessed that the exquisitely detailed toys were a gift from Linc to his niece.

''Linc, they're fabulous. Do you have others? How did you get started carving dolls? And what do you do with them, other than giving them to Tori?'' In her enthusiasm, her questions kept tumbling out.

"I have a few out in the tack room. I lived on the streets for a while after I split. A homeless man named Gus taught me to carve. He made dolls for his granddaughter, left them just inside the church doors a few blocks away. He figured the folks there knew how to get the gifts to heaven."

"Oh, no," Tracy Lynn whispered, her eyes tearing. "The girl died?"

He nodded. "A neighborhood kid threw her baby doll in the street and she went after it. The car that hit her never stopped. Gus was baby-sitting that day, and his son and daughter-in-law blamed him. He blamed himself, too. Spent every bit of money he had trying to track down the hit-and-run driver."

"And his kids just let him end up on the street?"

"You're very sheltered, babe. Families don't always treat each other nice."

"That's so sad. How long were *you* homeless?"

"Long enough to know I never want to be that way again."

She propped her elbows on the table, horrified at the hardships he must have endured, fascinated by this enigmatic man. "You're amazing. How did you go from living on the streets to becoming a filthy rich horse breeder?"

"Gambling." The corner of his mouth quirked upward when her eyes widened. "I worked on a couple of ranches in the area, and word spread that I was pretty good at cards. A city boy sat in on a game one day and anted the deed to an old dilapidated farm he'd inherited. Guess he figured he'd either make enough off me to pay the back taxes, or he'd get out from under it. I beat him with a royal flush and was happy to take the place off his hands.''

''You won a whole farm playing poker?'' She couldn't imagine something like that in today's society.

''Sure did. Jack loaned me some money to help pay the taxes. Then I started going to auctions and rescuing horses.''

''From what?''

''Slaughter.'' Her heart chilled when he said the word. ''I learned to recognize the killer buyers and outbid them. Even as the highest bidder, I still picked up the animals dirt cheap. One of my purchases was a maiden with champion Thoroughbred bloodlines. The bigger outfits steered clear of her because the owners listed her as barren. Imagine my surprise when she took a liking to my stallion and got herself pregnant.''

''Do you still rescue horses?''

''Yeah. I have the vet tend to them, give them some TLC, then when they're ready, I put them up for adoption.''

''For free?''

he nodded. ''To a good home. Some of the horses are old and weary. A lot of them have been neglected. Some are champion racehorses that have been injured and are no longer useful to their owners. They've still got life in them, though, and make fine pets or riding stock.''

''You mean people just get rid of them because

they can't perform? Or because they just don't want them anymore?'' Tracy Lynn was outraged.

''Pretty sad, huh?''

''I'd like to see one of those auctions. Although if I knew who the slaughter-minded creeps were, I doubt I could be held responsible for my actions.''

He chuckled and crossed his arms over his chest. ''There's an auction coming up the first of December. If you want, you can go with me. It would give you a chance to mingle a bit more with horses, help ease some of your fears.''

''Do you trust me not to start a brawl?''

His lips stretched in a sexy smile. ''I'll consider it my sworn duty to run interference. I spent time in jail once for fighting. You wouldn't like it.''

She nearly choked on her own breath. ''You went to jail?''

''Since I didn't have money for bail, there wasn't much choice.''

''I'm sorry, Linc, but if your father was here today, I'd slap the tar out of him.''

He chuckled. ''Babe, you wouldn't hurt a fly except by accident. But thanks for the offer.''

''You're welcome.'' She still felt livid on his behalf. But now that she gave her statement a bit more thought, she probably shouldn't have threatened violence, no matter how rhetorical, to a guy for whom violence had been a way of life.

''Did you ever find out what happened to Gus?''

''Yeah. He works for me.''

That caught her off guard. She was so touched, it

was a moment before she could speak. He helped a homeless man carve dolls for a little girl in heaven, plus rescued unwanted animals and pregnant women—at least one pregnant woman.

He was an absolute study in contrasts. Just looking at him when he got that stoic expression on his face was enough to scare a person off.

How had he ended up with such a streak of goodness when so much of his life was ruled by anger?

There were so many things she admired about this man, and the more she learned about him, the more she wished that somehow she could've married him first and then gotten pregnant with his child....

Determined not to linger on thoughts of things that couldn't be, she refocused on her original topic. "Okay, you like to play cards, gamble. How about billiards?"

He nodded. "Good idea. We've got plenty of room for a pool table."

Her pulse jumped. She waited another beat to see if his use of *we* had been intended or merely a figure of speech. His demeanor didn't change, and she realized that he wasn't even aware that he'd coupled them.

And she was being ridiculous, making way too much out of a simple word.

"Do you dance?" Wrong question. Her mind immediately snapped back to their wedding night, and what their slow dance had led to. She could tell by looking at Linc that he was sharing the same memory.

"Of course you dance," she corrected herself quickly with a laugh. "I meant, do you *like* to? Do you go out honky-tonkin'?"

"I don't make it a point to, no. Not enough spare time in my life." He shrugged. "But dancing's okay."

"So much enthusiasm," she drawled. "I *love* to dance."

His gray-blue eyes lifted lazily, locked onto hers. "Alone or with a partner?"

"Preferably with a partner." She had the feeling they were now talking about a different type of dance, and she was helpless to look away from his penetrating gaze.

Desire spread through her body. It would be so easy to melt into him and let nature take its course. But the words she'd flung at him in the barn came back to her. *What do you want from me? My word of honor that I won't try to entice you back into bed? Fine. You've got it.*

She didn't care for the idea of any man regretting that he'd made love to her. Especially Linc. If there was going to be a repeat of that awesome night, it would be up to him to make the first move. Meanwhile, Tracy Lynn needed some distance to cool off.

"Um, I think I've got enough information now to get started. I'd better clean up these dishes, though, and go to bed...to sleep, I mean." *Shut up, Tracy Lynn.* She hopped up and reached for the bowls.

Linc put his hand over hers. "Leave them. I've

got some phone calls to make, so I'll be up for a while. I'll take care of the kitchen.''

Before she talked herself out of it, she turned her hand over in his, gripped his palm and squeezed.

''I had a nice time tonight,'' she said. ''The two of us talking. You're a good man—don't frown at me like that. You are. Why can't we just continue to be this way together?''

His frown deepened and she pressed forward in her efforts to sway him. ''Thanksgiving is next week,'' she said, ''and then Christmas will be right on top of us. It's uncomfortable for both of us to tiptoe around each other when we're alone and don't have to pretend our marriage is real. Besides, I'm a people person, and I don't want to rattle around in this big house all by myself. I need somebody to talk to at the end of the day. Would it be so difficult to just be pals?''

His brow shifted, whether in surprise or horror, she wasn't sure.

''You're a gorgeous woman, babe. Being just pals is a tall order.''

''Oh, don't be such a *guy*. Ignore the outside package and just hang out with me once in a while. There are going to be furniture decisions we need to make, parties to attend, gifts to buy. I'll need help putting up the tree. We could at least give it a try. Just until after the holidays. By then, Daddy should be on the mend, and we'll get everything out in the open.''

He studied her for a long moment, then finally nodded. ''Okay. Consider me the boy next door.''

She laughed and shifted their palms so they could shake on the deal. "I think I'll stick to housemate. It's much more credible."

LINC STEPPED OUTSIDE the hay barn and saw Tracy Lynn's red Mustang streaking down the road that led from Jack's end of the property to his own. He absently scratched Buck's ears as the dog sat patiently at his side. What the heck was she up to now?

In the week since their marriage, he'd hardly gotten any work done because he was too busy watching Tracy Lynn's comings and goings. It was a darn good thing he'd hired extra help. Once he'd gotten the word out that the Royal Flush, his horse-breeding operation in Dallas, had branched out and partnered with the Forked S here in Hope Valley, business had been hopping.

But lately his concentration ranged from very little to none. No wonder. Delivery trucks arrived daily to drop off furniture, and construction vehicles crowded his driveway. The house was brand-new, yet Tracy Lynn had carpenters in spewing sawdust everywhere and putting up decorative moldings, while painting crews repainted the walls with fancy textures.

She was at the hospital every day, yet still managed to order furniture and drapes, and charm construction workers into performing miracles.

He'd say one thing for her. When she set her mind to getting something done, everybody shifted into high gear.

Although his libido kept him in a constant state of

tension, he liked having her in his house, like talking to her at the end of the day, learning the latest news from the hospital or at Donetta's Secret, which she also managed to visit every day or so.

She was ultrafeminine, which showed in her frequent trips to the salon, her manicured fingers and toenails, the mouth-watering scent that lingered in the bathroom after she showered, the perfumed lotion she slathered on her skin.

As the sports car barreled closer, he could hear her stereo blasting. He squinted against the sunlight, realizing she wasn't alone in the vehicle.

"What the...?" His mouth dropped open. Tori was riding shotgun, and two huge dogs were sitting politely in the back seat, their ears flapping in the wind.

Man alive, he needed a camera.

She brought the car to a stop right next to him, turned down the stereo's volume and beamed a smile that threatened to knock the air out of his lungs.

"I don't think the neighbors are going to appreciate you doing the dogcatcher's job, babe. Besides, one of those animals happens to be a police officer." The German shepherd, Dixie, in the back seat belonged to Storm Carmichael, the sheriff. As did the little rat terrier, Sneak, that Tori was holding in the front seat. The other hound, Simba, was related to Linc by Jack's marriage to Sunny.

Tracy Lynn laughed. "*Retired* officer. Can I borrow Buck for the day?"

"You've got two dogs the size of small horses

plus a little runt. What are you going to do with another hundred-pound animal?''

''We're going to visit the seniors, Uncle Linc,'' Tori said. ''They like to see kids and animals. It makes them happy. And we have to help them get ready for Thanksgiving. We have pumpkins and flowers in the trunk to make pretty table pieces.''

''I see. Are the dogs going to help out with arts and crafts?''

''No, silly. They're for petting and kisses.''

''Hmm. How come you're not in school?''

''Because some plumbing broke and we don't have any water in the bathrooms and drinking fountains.''

''Guess that's a good enough reason.'' Linc looked down at Buck. ''What do you say, boy? Are you up for petting and kisses?'' Buck gave a happy bark, which caused Simba to hang over the side of the car in excitement and return the greeting. Sneak scrambled out of Tori's arms, leaped into Tracy Lynn's lap and put her paws on the door to see what all the fuss was about. To her credit—and training—Dixie stayed where she was, giving the other two dogs a disgusted look.

What a sight. Leave it to Tracy Lynn not to do anything in a small way.

''Babe, I'm not so sure you and Tori can handle all these dogs by yourselves.''

''Of course we can. But just in case, why don't you come with us?''

''Yeah, Uncle Linc. Come with us.''

''We won't all fit in that speeding metal steed of yours.'' He couldn't believe the idea actually appealed to him. He'd never once stepped foot in a seniors' center. ''We'd have to take my Suburban.''

''Nonsense. We don't have that far to go, and it would be silly to unload my trunk twice.'' She gathered Sneak in one arm, opened the driver's door and leaned forward so the seat back bent with her. ''Come on, Buck. Get in. Tori, sweetie, hop in the back seat and buckle up. Dixie, Simba, lie down. Oh, that's a good boy, Buck,'' she praised the Lab when he obeyed, as well. ''Don't squish Tori, Simba. There you go.''

Amazed, Linc watched the shuffle take place, then looked into Tracy Lynn's I-told-you-so dancing eyes. He shook his head. He should have known she would one-up him.

''All right, I'll go. But *I'm* driving. I want to get there in one piece.''

Chapter Nine

Linc kept a sharp eye on the little old lady inching closer to him. Bitsy Jeeter was her name—she'd told him so just before she'd patted him on the behind.

Good God Almighty, the woman was old enough to be his *great*-grandmother. If she took one more step, he was going to run like the devil.

Hope Valley Convalescent Home offered both independent living and "skilled care" facilities, so there was a diverse group of people wandering around. The seniors' center was a fairly new gymnasium-size addition to the complex, providing the residents with a second dining hall that also doubled as an activities room.

He wasn't quite sure how he'd been roped into gutting pumpkins so they could be used as bowls for the floral centerpiece project. Probably because he was the only one with steady-enough hands who could be trusted with a knife.

"Want me to help you scoop the seeds, Uncle Linc?" Tori asked as she joined him in the kitchenette that was open to the rest of the room.

He looked down at the front of his shirt, now decorated with slimy strings of orange. "Heck, yes. But we'd better find you an apron. Your mama'll skin me alive if I let you mess up your pretty sweater."

"Naw." Tori grinned up at him. "She don't really skin people. She just threatens Daddy."

Linc figured his brother could handle himself pretty well. Jack had been in love with Sunny since high school—although he'd screwed up royally and lost her for ten years. Thank God he'd gotten a second chance. Jack was a different person these days, and one would never guess that Sunny wasn't Tori's biological mother. They were the quintessential perfect family in Linc's eyes, and one of the major reasons he was back in Hope Valley.

Because deep down, he wanted what Jack and Sunny had.

He wanted a family.

"Come here, doll." An older woman beckoned to Tori from her wheelchair. "I'll fix you up with this napkin. We'll tuck it in like the Italians do when they eat their spaghetti."

Tori danced over to the lady and allowed herself to be bibbed. "Uh-oh."

"Uh-oh, what?" Linc spun around to see what was wrong now. He'd already had to hide the extra knives in his hip pocket—and had nearly forgotten once and sat down on them.

"Sneak's got somebody else's slippers," Tori said. "Sorry, Uncle Linc. I better go get them."

She charged off after the mischievous dog, leaving

Linc at the table with four smiling grandmas breathing down his neck as they impatiently waited for their pumpkins.

That was the third pair of slippers Sneak had stolen. Usually Dixie ran herd on the terrier, but the shepherd was busy being lavished with affection by several of the other residents. He had no idea where Buck had gotten off to, but was confident the Lab would mind his manners. Surprisingly, Simba wasn't doing too badly either, other than knocking over a stack of folding chairs with his enthusiastically wagging tail.

Linc hadn't realized the dogs would have the run of the place. He'd thought Tracy Lynn and Tori would leash them and walk them from room to room, which was why he'd worried they couldn't handle Scooby-Doo and company on their own.

"How's it going in here?" Tracy Lynn asked as she breezed into the kitchenette area.

Linc whipped around and glared. It wasn't bad enough that he was being rushed by a bunch of sweet little old ladies—now Tracy Lynn was getting in on the act? "I'm cutting and scooping as fast as I can."

"And you're doing an excellent job."

The smile on her face flat out captivated him.

She pushed up her sleeves and, using a long handle spoon, scooped out the insides of the pumpkin he'd just cut the top off of. "I think we've got enough pumpkins now. Janie—" she turned to a tiny woman wearing neon-orange exercise clothes

"—why don't you take your flowers and your group over to Alma's table, and I'll bring the pumpkins."

The ladies who'd been eagerly watching his every move—as well as the one who'd asked to *see* his moves—gathered their things and assembled at one of the round tables in the dining hall. Linc barely curbed an urge to sigh. This was worse pressure than supervising an expensive stallion covering a temperamental mare.

"Thanks, Linc," Tracy Lynn said. "You've been a trooper." She shoved a green florist's cube into the pumpkin he'd been working on and took it right out from under him.

"Yeah, well, we'll draw straws to see who has to pull laundry duty."

She gave him a seriously bewildered look. "You do your own laundry?"

"Most of the time. Don't you?"

"No." She laughed softly. "You probably don't want me to start, either, at least not on your clothes. I'll ask Suelinda to recommend someone." She patted the small of his back, then frowned and lifted his shirt hem. "Linc, why do you have knives in your hip pocket?"

"I'm saving Curtis from a trip to the hospital." He nodded to the skinny gentleman who was now in a hot game of checkers. "The man has a thing for sharp items. Have you seen the way his hands shake?"

She smiled. "Actually, you and Curtis have something in common. He made a pretty decent name for himself over in Fredericksburg for his carvings of mockingbirds and falcons. Not only are you a trooper, you're a sweetheart to watch out for him."

"Don't go assigning me frilly titles. My choice of hiding place is purely self-serving—I'm protecting myself from Bitsy Jeeter's wandering hands. Every time she passes behind me she cops a feel of my butt."

Tracy Lynn laughed. "Linc, that's not very nice of you to deny Bitsy the memory of a firm, sexy derriere. She's ninety-one. I'd say she's earned a squeeze or two."

"You think my derriere's sexy?" He made a valiant effort to keep the smile from his face.

"Absolutely." She batted her eyelashes, her blue eyes dancing with amusement.

He lost the battle with his smile. Sassy woman. He hadn't expected her to admit that so openly—and she'd known it.

"Just a friendly warning," she said, gathering a second pumpkin in her arms, "Bitsy's curiosity doesn't limit itself to only backsides. So if I were you, I wouldn't be putting sharp instruments down the front of my pants."

Grinning, she flitted away and left him standing there with pumpkin slime still coating his fingers, thoroughly charmed.

He shook his head, then washed his hands and began cleaning up the mess, all the while keeping an eye on Tracy Lynn.

He was amazed at her gentleness with the elderly.

Because she came from a wealthy, prominent family, sometimes people made the mistake of judging her by the outside package—a pampered beauty queen with a dynamite body who caught the eye of every man she passed. Hell, even he'd been guilty of typecasting her.

But he was beginning to see that she had much deeper layers.

Not wanting to appear so obvious about watching her, Linc cut the pumpkin remains into squares and sketched the outline of a turkey on each one.

He reached into his pocket for his knife, then sat facing the dining room and began to shave and shape the orange squash, his gaze alternating between his project and Tracy Lynn. She'd always been a fantasy, but now she was like a drug in his system. He was hooked.

He listened as she discussed recipes and memories of Thanksgivings past with Alma and Janie's group, her hands busily arranging fresh flowers in the pumpkin centerpieces. With grace and poise, she moved around the room, stopping to help with a crossword puzzle, cheering over a game of dominoes, sitting in on a hand of bridge when someone had to use the rest room.

There was something enchanting about the way she tossed her head when she talked, like a colt who was enjoying life.

One of the ladies noticed Tracy Lynn's wedding ring, and the conversational noise level in the room increased to an excited buzz. His fingers tightened around the hilt of the knife as her gaze connected with his.

For an instant she appeared worried.

And then she smiled. A smile so inclusive, so intimate, it settled against his heart like a loving caress.

Which was really stupid. They were in a public place. Both were honorbound to play the role of newlyweds.

She looked like a supermodel, yet she had old-fashioned ideas and miles of compassion. Honesty and being a truly genuine person came naturally to her. So he knew how hard it was for her to lie to all these good people.

Unable to hold her gaze, he looked away and saw that Curtis was no longer playing checkers. Instead, the man was watching him. Longingly.

Linc tossed his head in a gesture that invited the man to join him.

"I heard you carve birds," he said when Curtis drew near.

Curtis pulled out a chair across from him and sat down. "Used to before I had me a stroke and my hands took to shakin' like a hound dog passin' a peach pit."

Linc winced. "Man, I've seen that before. Your hands don't look quite that bad to me. You still do any carving?"

Curtis shook his head. "My girls took away my tools, scared I'd cut off a finger or somethin'."

Ah, hell. "What do you think?"

"They're worrywarts. 'Course, I don't really have

the strength anymore to work with hardwoods. What are you makin' there?''

''Turkeys. Figured the ladies could stick them in their flower arrangements.''

''How'd you reckon on makin' 'em stand up in the flowers?''

Linc shrugged. ''Maybe a fork. I'm not sure. You have any suggestions?''

''Hmm. We've got some of them long matchsticks in the drawer over there. Use 'em to light the stove when the propane runs low, but I don't reckon any-body'd get too riled if you borrowed a few. Be sturdy enough to stick in the pumpkin meat, and the other end'd poke down real good in the florist's cube.''

''There you go. How much trouble do you suppose we'll get in if I turn you loose with a knife?''

Curtis's eyes lit up. ''You look like a fella who could hold his own pretty good if somebody kicked up a fuss. Me? I'll just put on a blank stare and let you take the fall.''

Linc grinned. Figuring there'd be less chance of bloodletting if he was the one who made do with the kitchen paring knife, he passed his own pocketknife to the older man along with a block of pumpkin. A master carver deserved a topnotch tool.

''Watch yourself, now. I'm liable to pass out at the sight of blood.''

Curtis laughed. ''You just tend to your own whit-tlin'. And don't be rushin' the job, neither. Long as you stay busy, won't nobody rope you into readin' to the folks whose eyesight's poor. Boy, you don't want to go there."

"Why's that?"

"'Cuz your wife's got her own ideas on reading material, and you only get three choices."

Your wife. Linc's insides jolted and the paring knife slipped, barely missing his knuckle.

"Romance novels," Curtis continued, "because she says they give hope and always have a happy ending."

"She's a 'glass half full' kind of gal," Linc said.

"I reckon she is. Poetry and the Psalms are the other two, because they're beautiful, accordin' to Tracy Lynn." Curtis laid down a perfectly carved turkey and picked up another block of pumpkin.

"I can't see what all the fuss is about," he continued. "'Course, them poems aren't exactly my cup of coffee. 'Bout get the hang of that rhymin' business, then they go and toss in a sucker line that fouls up the whole works. I get so durn caught up in the last word on each line to where I've got no idea a'tall what the blazes I just read. And the Psalms…seems like every time I'm pressed into reading service, it falls durin' a week I missed church. Just pickin' up that Bible tends to make me feel like a sinner."

Linc smiled. He figured Curtis hadn't had a chance to air out his thoughts in a while. And even though the man's hands trembled, he was whittling three turkeys to Linc's one.

"Does Tracy Lynn come here often?"

"Yes siree. Every week. We wouldn't know what

to do without her. That girl's one that keeps her promises, too.''

Linc's heart squeezed. Her dedication to the seniors was another reminder that her roots were firmly planted in Hope Valley's soil. Technically, his were, too, but they were damaged. Which didn't bode well for happy endings. At least not for him.

He didn't know why he was wasting his time thinking about this, anyway. Jerald Randolph was being released from the hospital tomorrow and Tracy Lynn would likely move back home to take care of him. In which case, she'd have ample opportunities to level with her father about the baby, and there would no longer be a reason to stay married.

His paring knife sliced right through the pumpkin and lobbed off the turkey's head.

''Don't look down, son,'' Curtis said. ''Your turkey's done had its neck wrung, and I'd sure hate to see you pass out on the floor and embarrass yourself. Especially in front of the pretty ladies that just walked in the door.''

TRACY LYNN WAS DELIGHTED to see Linc spending time with Curtis. She wasn't sure what they were carving, but she hadn't seen Curtis this animated in the entire year he'd been living here.

She'd started to wander over in their direction when Donetta breezed through the door, hauling a suitcase that Tracy Lynn knew contained hair and fingernail products. Right behind her was Abbe Shea, holding the hand of her three-year-old daughter, Jolene.

''Good thing I'm not fixing Thanksgiving dinner,'' Donetta said, flicking her long red hair behind her shoulder. ''I'd never get the preparations done in time.''

''Today's Tuesday, Donetta.'' Tracy Lynn and Linc's one-week anniversary. ''Thanksgiving isn't until Thursday.''

''Obviously you've never cooked for a crowd. Anna said to tell you she'll be bringing the meal *and* the guests over to your daddy's house since he probably won't be up to traveling.'' Donetta's gaze shifted. ''Hey, handsome.''

Tracy Lynn gave a start when she realized Linc was standing behind her.

''Hey, yourself, Donetta. Hi, Abbe.''

''Oh, Lordy. Abbe, get up here. You're so quiet, I nearly forgot you were here. Abbe had the misfortune to be my last customer before lunch,'' Donetta said, looking at Linc. ''Tracy Lynn called me in such a panic I twisted Abbe's arm and dragged her along to paint fingernails.''

''Thank you for coming, Abbe,'' Tracy Lynn said. ''You look fabulous as usual.'' Abbe Shea was a truly stunning woman. She wore her blond hair in a short, sassy style that accentuated her high cheekbones and large eyes.

And she was a puzzle, as well. Tracy Lynn wasn't sure if it was shyness, or if Abbe just liked to keep to herself, but no one really knew much about her except that she'd left town years ago, then quietly reappeared with a child a few months back.

"And, Jolene," Tracy Lynn said, "you sweet thing. Who put those cute puppy-dog ears in your hair?"

"They're *pig*tails!" Jolene giggled and hopped from foot to foot. Not a shy bone in her body.

"Donetta said you had an emergency?" Abbe asked.

"A slight one," Tracy Lynn confirmed. "Last week I asked Donetta to come out here and fix up the ladies' hair and nails—just as a favor to me. I thought it'd be a treat. I guess they got the impression it was a new weekly event, and there's already been two shoving and hair-pulling incidents over the sign-up sheet."

Tracy Lynn looked at Donetta and continued, "I'm sorry, Netta. I had no idea. I'll be forever indebted to you both if you'll help me out of this bind before one of the ladies ends up in a brawl."

"I love it when you're indebted to me," Donetta said cheerfully. "Maybe we should start a tab. First you conned me out of my dogs— Where are they, by the way?"

"The last time I saw them, they were down the hall with the residents in skilled care."

"Actually," Linc said, "I was just on my way to check on them. Sneak seems to have developed a slipper fetish."

"Oh, isn't she the cutest thing?" Donetta laughed, unconcerned that her dog by marriage was showing serious signs of kleptomania. ''Come on, Abbe. Let's go referee these feisty gals and pull Tracy Lynn's fat out of the fire.''

''Let's don't get started on anybody's fat,'' Tracy Lynn warned.

Donetta just laughed.

As soon as the residents spotted Donetta and Abbe, they abandoned flowers, cards and dominoes in a mad rush across the room, a couple of them even breaking into a run.

''Honestly,'' Tracy Lynn said. ''The sign-up sheet determines the order of the appointments. You'd think they were all competing for the last box of oatmeal on special at the Piggly Wiggly.''

''Crazy,'' Linc agreed with a chuckle. ''Did you just see Bitsy throw out an arm block and cut in front of Janie?''

''She probably learned that move back in the days when she roller-skated with the Thunderbirds, in which case, we're lucky she didn't bloody Janie's nose. I watched a tape of Bitsy's televised roller derbies, and the woman can certainly hold her own.''

''I'm not familiar with roller derby.''

''Think WWF wrestlers, hockey players and Hooters. Put those images together and you've got women in tight T-shirts and short-shorts racing around an oval track on roller skates, deliberately antagonizing the other team—no holds barred.''

''Well, I'll be damned. Maybe I should have given her proposition more thought.''

Tracy Lynn elbowed him in the ribs. ''Sugar,

you're more man than most women can handle, but Bitsy Jeeter would chew you up and spit you out.''

''Babe. She's ninety-one.''

Tracy Lynn shrugged. ''She put the moves on Daddy once and scared him half to death. Had him backed into the storage closet before he even knew what hit him.''

Linc laughed and hooked his arm around her neck, drawing stares and smiles from several people. Tracy Lynn could just imagine what they were thinking. *Oh, how sweet. Newlyweds.*

If they only knew, she thought.

But Linc's spontaneous affection didn't feel like an act. Since the night of her father's surgery, they'd truly become friends. Oh, there was still the crackle of sexual tension that got in the way—especially when they bumped into each other in their pajamas, or eyeballed the placement of a new bed she'd ordered for one of the five bedrooms.

She might have compared their relationship to a real marriage—except they didn't sleep together.

''I'd like to see that tape,'' Linc said.

''Forget it. You're already too enamored.''

''Jealous?''

''In your dreams, cowboy. I'm simply doing a good deed and saving your masculine dignity.''

''Babe. If you're worried about my stamina and self-confidence in the bedroom, I'm going to rethink these cold showers I've been taking since our wedding night. Clearly, I didn't make a strong-enough impression.''

Oh, she'd blundered right into this one. Or had it been deliberate?

For the first time in her life, she'd found a man she responded to on every level, yet they'd erected fair-play rules between them. And in that respect, Tracy Lynn had quite a bit in common with Betsy Jeeter. Because when it came to Lincoln Slade, she was inclined to step into the foul zone and worry about the penalty later.

But not in the middle of the seniors' center.

He still had his arm around her neck, though now his gaze had shifted to her mouth.

Someone started clinking the glassware. Next came the sound of silverware tapping on the tables. The noise grew. Tracy Lynn looked over at Donetta, who was grinning.

"What is she thinking? This isn't a wedding reception!"

"Maybe not," Linc said. "But, babe, when utensils are banging on glass and we're the only ones not participating, I figure that's our cue to kiss." With a finger beneath her chin, he turned her face to his and did just that.

For several moments, Tracy Lynn heard nothing but the beat of her own heart. He gave her an open-mouthed kiss that involved only their lips, a kiss so perfect she could hardly recall her own name.

She realized that in the past, kissing was a part of intimacy she hadn't enjoyed all that much. She'd never admitted that before, had always felt that something was wrong with her.

Clearly, she just hadn't been kissing the right man.

When he lifted his head, it took her a couple of

seconds to gather her senses. At last reality broke through the fog and she immediately started to pull away, but he tightened his hold, keeping her in place for a moment longer as their audience applauded. Then he pressed his lips to her forehead and let her go.

She'd never had so much trouble reading a man's signals. His touch felt a lot like love. Yet his actions didn't exactly follow. Could their pretense be turning into reality? Or was she simply seeing things that weren't there?

Since she didn't have that answer, she had to heed her instincts, rein in her natural tendencies to leap before looking, or to see a silver lining where there was none. She wasn't going to embarrass either of them by assuming too much.

She looked toward the makeshift beauty shop. Donetta was styling Alma's hair, while Abbe painted Janie's nails. The line of ladies waiting their turn looked daunting.

"Now I feel bad for Donetta. She's pregnant, and I'm sure she gets tired easily. Maybe I should go over there and help."

"You're pregnant, too, babe."

"Yes, but she's farther along than I am. And she suffered for several months with horrible morning sickness. Actually, it was more like all-day and all-night nausea. If Storm hadn't been able to heal her with hypnosis, she'd really be miserable."

"Have you had any morning sickness?"

"Not yet. Knock on wood." She rapped her knuckles against the table next to them. "If and when

I do, I'm going right over to Storm's house to be hypnotized.''

''When did the sheriff start dabbling in that kind of stuff?''

''Since the Texas Rangers sent him to classes to teach him. They use hypnosis in forensics to help solve cases.''

''Hmm. Sure come a long way, haven't they?''

''Yes.'' As though they figured it would make their turn come faster, the ladies kept inching their chairs closer to the primping area. Soon Abbe and Donetta weren't going to have any room to maneuver. ''Do you think Abbe's shy?''

''I don't know much about her. I suppose she could be.''

''I don't remember her being that way in school.''

''People change.''

''Maybe. There's something more, though. It's as if she's hiding—from what or whom, I don't have a clue. And she's so protective of Jolene.''

''Who's the father?''

''She's never said. She still has her maiden name, so I don't know if she was even married.''

''She must have money coming in from somewhere,'' Linc said. ''She keeps a twin engine Beechcraft out at the airport.''

''See there. How many women in Hope Valley do you know who fly their own airplane? She probably needs it in case she has to make a fast getaway.''

Linc chuckled. ''Your imagination is working overtime.'' He stroked a fingertip lightly over her cheek. ''You have a special gift when it comes to people and compassion. But you can't fix everyone, babe.'' His voice softened. ''Sometimes happy endings just aren't possible.''

She had an idea they were no longer talking about Abbe. Here again was the confusion over his actions and his words.

''I don't believe that,'' she said.

''Of course you don't. You think there's a solution to every problem, right? You just need to figure out who to call.''

Had she just been insulted? His summation of her character made her sound like a ditz. Maybe she did have a touch of Pollyanna in her, but she'd rather be that way than pessimistic about life.

Moments ago, she'd cautioned herself not to search for silver linings. But that went against who she was at her core.

''Everyone has to have hope, Linc. Life is about possibilities. If I didn't believe that, I wouldn't have this baby in my womb.'' She lifted his hand and kissed his knuckles. As his eyebrows rose in surprise, she turned and walked away.

Granted, reaching for what she wanted had caused conflicts she hadn't expected, turned her entire world upside down. But hope and believing in the possibilities of what her future could bring, and for this baby that she wanted more than anything, was what kept her strong.

Chapter Ten

Through the front windows of the small Italian bistro where they'd just finished having dinner, Linc kept an eye on Tori as she skipped along the sidewalk and hopped into the back seat of the Mustang to feed Simba and Buck their specially made doggie pizzas. To cheer them up, she'd said, since Sneak and Dixie had ridden home with Donetta.

He'd given Tori permission to go back to the car ahead of them while he and Tracy Lynn settled the bill, an event that was beginning to look as though it might become a major battle.

Standing, he put on his jacket. "Don't bother getting into your purse, Tracy Lynn. You're *not* paying for dinner."

"Oh, yes, I am." She slid out of the red vinyl booth and bolted.

His jaw dropped.

Okay, this was a first—even for him. He'd never before had a foot race with a woman in a restaurant. Especially when picking up the tab was the winner's prize.

He caught her in two strides, snagged her around the waist and set her behind him, easily gaining the lead.

"That's cheating," she said, trying to skirt around him.

Amusement replacing his initial astonishment, he blocked her access to the cash register, trying not to gloat.

"Would you please move out of my way?" Her tone was excruciatingly polite with a subtle edge of growing irritation.

Grinning, he pulled his wallet from his back pocket, then chuckled when Tracy Lynn clapped both her hands over his, presumably to prevent him from getting to his money.

"Babe. Do you really think you'll win in a tug-of-war against me? Not to mention the scene it'll cause."

"Don't let this well-mannered exterior fool you." She lifted her chin. "Donetta gave all of us Sweethearts a lesson in brawling—just in case a necessary occasion ever arose, you understand."

Linc bit the inside of his cheek and cleared his throat. The urge to laugh was nearly killing him. "Is that so?"

"Absolutely. Now, since I issued the invitation to supper, I intend to treat, so you may as well move. Besides, I ordered extra food."

"You didn't get enough to eat?" He gave an experimental tug on his wallet. She hung on like a terrier.

The boy working the counter walked up and set two large, boxed pizzas next to the cash register.

"I had plenty to eat. Really, Linc. I *have* to pay. Otherwise, I might have to tell a lie."

"A...?" Her statement was so outrageous, he was helpless to suppress his burst of laughter, which gave her the edge to squeeze in front of him.

She opened her purse and addressed the boy behind the cash register. "If that hyena behind me tries to muscle his way in, do *not* take his money. Understand?"

"Yes'm."

"Honestly," she muttered. "You men. Half the time you act like Neanderthals." She pinned the young clerk with a direct glare. "Do you have a girlfriend?"

"Uh...yes ma'am."

"Well, if she offers to buy you a meal, I expect you to give in gracefully and allow her to do so."

"Yes, ma'am."

She slapped several bills on the counter. "Do I look old to you?"

Uh-oh, Linc thought. He knew that tone. And the distressed expression on the poor kid's face started him laughing all over again.

"No, ma'am."

"Then *why* do you keep calling me *ma'am?*"

"Uh, policy, ma'am."

Linc put his wallet back in his hip pocket and took pity on the innocent pizza clerk. Sliding his arm around Tracy Lynn's shoulders, he winked at the kid.

"Her birthday's coming up Christmas Eve. Touchy subject. Who are you going to lie to, babe?"

"I'm not touchy about my birthday. I might have been, though, if I hadn't gotten pregnant."

Tom, according to his name tag, stopped in the middle of counting change. Sweating now, he sighed and started over for the third time.

"And I don't have to lie to Hardy Pederson now...I don't think," she added. "The feed-supply company he was working for went out of business. I'm buying the pizzas for his family. It's tough when you've got a wife and three kids to support and no job—one of those kids happens to be a playmate of Tori's. Plus, Hardy's a proud man and doesn't want charity, so I might have to be a little inventive when I stop by with supper."

"What excuse were you thinking about using? Might as well give it a test drive on me."

"I thought I'd simply tell him that I'd ordered more food than my dinner guests could eat, and that I remembered how much little Annie—Tori's pal—loves pizza."

"What if they've already eaten?"

"Then they'll have a couple more nights where they don't have to worry about the menu. Pizzas freeze very nicely."

"So, why can't you freeze them? They wouldn't go to waste then."

She folded her arms beneath her breasts. "Daddy's coming home from the hospital and he doesn't like pizza. Plus, I'm sure it's not a recommended item on the cardiac diet.''

He nodded. ''Okay. It flies.''

She smiled, clearly pleased. ''I figured we'd drop off Tori and Simba, then I can take you back to the house and go on over to the Pedersons' place.''

''Where do they live?''

''In the trailer park out by Bear Creek Road. It's not far from the house.''

''I've got a better idea,'' he said. ''We'll take Tori home, then I'll go with you to the Pedersons'.''

''You don't have to do that.'' Tom finally managed to count out her change. She stuffed it in her purse, thanked him sweetly and reached for the pizza boxes. ''You've got to be worn out after today.''

''Me? You're the one whose tail ought to be dragging.'' He plucked the warm cardboard containers out of her hands. ''Thanks, buddy,'' he said to the clerk, then pushed open the door with his free hand so she could precede him outside.

Truthfully, he was amazed at her energy. He was in condition for twelve-hour days of physical work, but spending a mere five hours at a seniors' center had him longing for home, his TV remote and his leather recliner. He'd never admit that, of course.

Especially since Tracy Lynn didn't look a bit wilted. Hell, she'd probably phone all her friends to catch up on their lives, go visit her father in the hospital, then hang drapes and rearrange furniture—*after* delivering supper to a family down on their luck.

''I'm beginning to see why you haven't gotten

married before now,'' he said, pausing by the hood of her car. ''You don't have time for a social life.''

''On the contrary,'' she said, laughing, ''I have plenty of time. And I lead quite an active social life, thank you very much. Although that's not always a good thing for a person who sometimes has the memory recall of a gnat. I've been guilty of double-booking my calendar.''

He glanced in the car, saw that Tori was content feeding the dogs. ''Then what's been the holdup in relationships?''

She shrugged. ''I never found anyone I truly clicked with. I was in a relationship three years ago with an attorney who worked here in town, but he couldn't get past the fact that I had a bigger bank account than he did. So, he took his law degree, along with one of the preschool teachers from the Gingerbread House, and moved to Colorado.''

''Guy must have had cow pies for brains. Did he break your heart?''

She shook her head. ''I thought so at first. Then I realized I was mostly upset that he'd cheated on me with the teacher. As for the rest of my unproductive dating life, the money issue has been a problem. It seems the guys I've gone out with are either intimidated by me, or they only want sex and a trophy on their arm.'' She stepped off the curb and moved to the passenger door. ''No one has ever really taken the time to look past the surface to see what I'm all about.''

Linc hit the remote button to pop the trunk. Certainly *he* was looking.

He could understand how any man would be stunned initially when meeting her. She was one of the most beautiful women he'd ever laid eyes on, but once he'd pried his chin off his chest and screwed his eyes back in his head, Tracy Lynn's exterior package became only a small part of what Linc noticed when he looked at her. He mostly saw the heart of her. She was good and kind and generous—not just with money, but with herself and her time.

And it was beginning to worry him how much he *did* see, how much about her he admired…and how much she made him feel.

He put the pizzas in the trunk, then got in the car. Once they were on the road, Tracy Lynn fiddled with the buttons on the CD player and the heater. She kept Tori entertained by singing along with Shania Twain, and sentenced him to a ten-mile ride in a moving sauna, making him sorry he'd raised the convertible top when they'd left the seniors' center.

By the time they reached his brother's house to drop off Tori and Simba, Linc was sure he'd sweated off five pounds. And he was also sure that Tracy Lynn was going to be one hell of a good mother.

"Daddy's truck's not here," Tori said. "I bet Uncle Storm needed him to go be a reserve deputy." There was a time when Jack's absence would have sent Tori into a frightened silence. Now she reacted matter-of-factly, like any other kid who was secure in her world. A lot of that had been Sunny's doing.

"I sure hope it's not a school bus wreck like the one I was in."

"There was no school today, kiddo," Tracy Lynn said. "Remember? Plus, it's dark. What school bus in its right mind would be caught running up and down the road at night?"

"Busses don't have minds," Tori said, giggling.

"Ha. Out you go, Miss Smarty Pants. Simba! Honestly, wait your turn." Tracy Lynn ducked her head back in the car. "Are you coming in?"

Linc shook his head. "I think I'll let Buck water the trees before we head off to our Meals On Wheels delivery."

She hesitated, her eyes boring into his as though she could see into his soul. "Well, tell him to hurry. I'll be right back."

While Buck hopped out to do his business, Linc shucked his jacket and stood beside the open car door to cool off.

The lights were on in the bunkhouse, the cattle settled in for the night. Mingling with the smell of animals and lush earth was the gentle scent of jasmine and roses from the flower garden by the front porch. That patch of ground had been his mother's pride and joy. After she died, Jack had tended the flowers and kept them flourishing.

Now that Linc thought about it, the garden was pretty much the only thing about this place that was recognizable from what it had been before. That and the abandoned shed-row stable over by the gravel turnoff. Although that road was the shortest route to the highway, Linc never used it.

He reached back inside the Mustang, switched the ignition key to Auxiliary. Hoping Tracy Lynn wouldn't notice, he turned down the heater.

A feminine shriek pierced the air. He rose up so fast, he cracked his head on the roof.

Arms flailing, Tracy Lynn darted off the porch as Sunny doubled over laughing.

"It's only a little spiderweb, Tracy Lynn," Sunny called.

Linc's heartbeat settled and he grinned, watching as she ran straight for the car.

"I *hate* spiders! Ew!" She slapped at her hair and her arms, then glared at Linc. "And stop laughing at me, you goon. It wouldn't hurt you to sweep your porch once in a while."

Instead of jumping in the car as he'd expected, she raced around to his side, nearly knocking him over.

"Is anything in my hair?"

"Babe—"

"Just look! Hurry." She shivered and danced in place. "If you laugh, I'll make you walk home."

"I'm shaking already."

With the car door open, there was enough light for him to see that no insects were hitching a free ride. But he combed his fingers through her hair, anyway, lightly massaged her scalp, brushed at the backside of her sweater, was about to do the front…

His body responded accordingly, and if there'd been a bench seat in that Mustang instead of buckets and a center console, he probably would have laid her down and conducted an entirely different kind of inspection. Instead, he wrapped his arms around her and lifted her, holding her flush against his aching body.

She grabbed for his shoulders. "Linc! What are you doing?"

"Squashing spiders."

"Squa—?" She looked down at him, then giggled.

The uncharacteristic sound made him smile. "I didn't think it would be a good idea to pat down the front of your sweater with Sunny still standing at the door."

"Probably not. Why don't you holler at her and tell her to go inside?"

"Babe. I'm not putting my hands anywhere near the front of your sweater."

She giggled again, charming him. "That's not what I meant!"

"Good, because that's surely not acceptable behavior between pals." He smiled and just looked at her for the pure pleasure of it.

"I bet you didn't realize what you were getting into when you agreed to come with me today," she said. "I hope I didn't keep you away from any pressing work."

"If I hadn't been able to spare the time, I wouldn't have gone." *Liar.* "Besides, I've hired several more employees this past week. And if you'll turn my neck loose, maybe we'll get this pizza delivered before

Hardy Pederson goes to bed—in which case, I'll have an opportunity to hire one more.''

Instead of letting go, her arms tightened, her elated smile making his knees go weak.

''You'd give Hardy a job without ever meeting him?''

''I imagine I'll meet him when we get there, babe.''

She tugged on his hair. ''You know what I mean.''

''If he's looking for work, I can use the help. I figure if Pederson's someone you care enough to worry about, then he comes with a fine recommendation.''

''You are a fabulous man.'' She leaned in and kissed him, catching him off guard. It was a quick kiss, one of excitement and gratitude, and before his brain could signal his mouth to participate, she'd pulled back, her smile beaming.

He knew damned well he was playing with fire, but he couldn't seem to help himself. ''Do that again,'' he said. ''A little slower.''

Her lips parted and she gazed at him as though he'd just offered her a free trip to Paris. Without hesitation, she brought her mouth to his again.

His mind went blank and his body came alive as her tongue swept his lips, teasing, driving him mad. She kissed him like a woman utterly sure of her femininity and her effect on a man. He felt the hot edge of her hunger as she moaned deep in her throat, poured herself into a kiss that left him numb and shaking.

He plunged his fingers into her hair, angled her head, took everything she offered and gave back in kind. When at last she pulled away, she looked as stunned as he felt.

"Well." She cleared her throat. "I believe that went a little further than just pals."

He lowered her to the ground. He was an idiot to torture himself—and Tracy Lynn—this way. They'd agreed to stay together through the holidays, yet it could end as soon as tomorrow.

"I suppose we should make tracks," he said, his voice huskier than usual. "Weren't you planning to stop by the hospital tonight and see your dad?"

"Darn it! I told you I get caught up and forget stuff. Where's my cell phone?" She climbed into the car and crawled across the front seat, giving him a perfect view of her derriere in body-hugging black slacks. He groaned and looked skyward, tracking a jetliner.

"Room 314, please."

Linc looked down, caught the sparkle of the diamonds on her wedding band, twisted the horseshoe ring on his own finger. She'd settled sideways in the driver's bucket seat, her legs dangling close to where he stood by the open passenger-side door.

"Hey, Daddy. It's me. You doing okay?... Really? What did the doctor say?... Uh-huh... Uh-huh... Are you sure?... Yes, I know you'll need help when you get home. I'll..."

Linc braced himself. He wished he wasn't hearing this conversation. But the same way a witness at a gnarly crash couldn't look away, he couldn't stop himself from listening.

"Ellie?... But I thought— Oh... Well, I— Yes... Daddy, I was planning to— Okay, I'll be there to pick you up in the morning. Night... Love you, too."

She disconnected and looked up at him. "Well, that's pretty weird."

He raised his brows, inviting her to elaborate.

"Ellie's taking a leave of absence from the hospital. I guess Daddy talked her into coming to work for him—to take care of him until he's on his feet. He said he didn't want to intrude on our marriage since it's so new."

"He hasn't mentioned this before now?" Linc couldn't believe his heart was still beating. He'd been half expecting her to announce she was moving back in with her father.

"Not a word. And I tell you, I've been a wreck worrying about the whole thing. He's a terrible patient and he's been hounding the doctors to let him go home. I think it's too soon—he still gets dizzy when he sits up. I'd be scared to death if I had to be responsible for his health at this point."

"Didn't you say you took care of your mom?"

"That was different. Daddy needs someone who can keep him *alive* until his body's strong enough to take over. I knew Mama was dying. Taking care of her was mostly making sure she was as comfortable as possible, just being there for her...until the end." She pulled her lips between her teeth, her eyes filling.

Linc knelt next to the car, not knowing what to

say. He pinched the crease of her pants, rubbed the fabric between his fingers, waited.

"Sorry." She gave a watery laugh. "It's been ten years, but it still sneaks up on me."

"No need to apologize. My mom's been gone almost fifteen years, and I miss her every day."

Tracy Lynn reached out and cupped his cheek. "Oh, Linc. I wish things had been different. That I could've been there for you then."

There was a time when he would have considered her words merely an empty platitude, read them as pity. But after watching her this past week, getting to know her, learning her deeper layers, seeing her genuine caring today at the seniors' center, he knew she spoke from her heart.

TRACY LYNN LOOKED OUT the window and saw Sunny's Suburban pulling up to the back entrance of the house. She grinned when she noticed the Christmas wreath attached to the SUV's grill. Lord, she could hardly believe it was already December.

These past two weeks since her father had been released from the hospital, she and Linc had resumed their just-friends status, despite the kiss out by Jack's house and the obviously still-hot chemistry between them. The time since had been a whirlwind of shopping, decisions and deliveries.

Furnishing and accessorizing a house this large was a big job. Even she had cringed at the size of the bills coming in.

Linc never batted an eyelash, though. As she'd

hoped, it was the simple things he was most impressed with: the display case she'd filled with his carvings; and the framed photo of the first mare he'd bought, the horse that had started him on the road to success.

She opened the back door just as Sunny was about to knock. "Hey, girl. What are you doing over in this neck of the woods?"

"Linc phoned and asked me to come over and check out a couple of horses he's bringing in. He said one of them is in pretty bad shape."

"Oh, no. Now I'm glad I didn't go with him. He asked me last week, but Ellie called and said she had personal business to tend to today, so I had to take Daddy to a doctor's appointment."

"It probably worked out better for Jack to go with him, anyway, since they ended up needing both horse trailers." Sunny rubbed a leaf on the peace lily that rested on the granite breakfast bar, her eyes roaming over every corner of the room.

"Tracy Lynn, this place is gorgeous! I can hardly believe this is the same house I was in—what has it been? Three weeks ago?"

"Mmm-hmm." She twisted the wedding ring on her finger.

Out of habit—and pride—Tracy Lynn glanced around the room where beautiful Aubusson and Persian rugs dressed up the hardwood floors, pulling together groupings of sofas and chairs that invited guests to cozy up and chat. The predominantly neutral colors, along with the mix of both antique and traditional furniture, gave the house a restful, welcoming air, with subtle reds and pale gold accents lending a hint of spice.

"I knew you'd do a fabulous job," Sunny said. "Especially after seeing what you did with Jack's house before I came along."

"All I can say is thank goodness I got to it before you did. You'd have probably tacked up a picture of a cow on the wall and called it good."

Sunny laughed. "I may not have any fashion and decorating sense, but I've yet to meet an animal I can't diagnose and tend to. Hopefully, this mare Linc's bringing home won't ruin my stellar reputation."

"Is the horse that bad?"

"I talked to Jack after Linc phoned. He said Miss Helen—that's the horse—is pretty much just skin and bones."

"Oh, then it's a doubly good thing I wasn't there. I'd have torn up creation if I saw someone trying to pawn off an animal they hadn't taken care of. Can you imagine what Linc would have done if I'd started a brawl?"

"According to Jack, your husband did just that."

"He got in a fight?"

"Yep. I guess when he saw some sleazebag whipping a buckskin mare, his civilized manners took a hike and he laid the guy out in one punch."

"You're kidding."

"No. Then he shoved a hundred-dollar bill in the man's mouth and took the horse."

''Only a hundred dollars for a horse? Isn't that awfully cheap? I mean, what if the guy claims he was forced into selling at that price?''

''Oh, I doubt it. Men like that are cowards. Besides, Jack thinks Linc paid more than a horse in Miss Helen's condition is worth. The mare's been badly neglected, and they're not even sure she'll live.''

''Oh, my God.''

Sunny put a hand on Tracy Lynn's arm. ''It's sad, but if that's the case, Miss Helen is in the very best place she can be. Between Linc and me, we can make sure she goes with dignity and without pain.''

''Add my name to yours and Linc's,'' Tracy Lynn said. She rushed over to the window. ''I hear Linc's truck.'' Two pickups hauling horse trailers pulled up next to the stable.

''I better get my gear and head out there,'' Sunny said.

Tracy Lynn decided she'd tag along.

She didn't know enough about horses to be of any help, but she could certainly lend moral support.

And she was darn good at raising awareness for causes. Linc might have used his brawn to make a point. She would use her brain and her many contacts if it turned out the horse was in as bad a shape as Sunny indicated.

Deliberately harming an animal was a punishable offense. If Linc hadn't already taken care of the matter, she'd make sure Miss Helen's vile ex-owner was in jail by sundown.

Chapter Eleven

Linc checked his side mirrors as he backed the horse trailer close to the barn.

He flexed his hand on the steering wheel. His knuckles hurt like a son of a gun. Satisfaction and disgust warred within him over plowing his fist into the scumbag horse owner's face.

That tiny town in the Hill Country seemed an unlikely place to find a good horse sale, but it had one of the best reputations for quality stock. Which was why Linc had been surprised by the condition of the buckskin. Horses like that usually ended up at Saturday-night everything-goes sales.

The bastard who'd owned Miss Helen had been lucky in two respects: first, he'd stayed down after the first punch; second, Jack had been there, stepping in as the voice of reason, reminding Linc that there was an animal in need. Otherwise, the red haze blinding Linc's vision might not have lifted until the miserable excuse for a human being was nothing more than a bloody smear in the dirt.

And that scared the hell out of him.

He'd been protecting an animal, yes, but it was the rage inside him that still bothered him, the loss of control.

He drew in a calming breath. It had taken more than an hour to coax the mare into the trailer. If he tried to unload her now with anger radiating off him, he'd never succeed without one of them getting hurt.

As he got out of the truck and made his way back to the trailer, he saw Tracy Lynn standing about twenty feet away. She wore a bright yellow sweater, jeans and boots— nothing out of the ordinary—yet she made the casual ranch attire appear fancy. Like a champion Thoroughbred, Tracy Lynn's breeding clearly showed.

She was so obviously born to regal settings, he couldn't imagine her ever getting used to the dusty, earthy environment of a working ranch.

He dragged his attention away from Tracy Lynn as Sunny walked up to him. Jack joined them a moment later.

''Hey, sugar bear,'' Jack said, bending down to give his wife a kiss. Both Linc and Jack towered over the five-foot-three veterinarian—and both had the self-preservation not to comment on her lack of height. Riled up, or around animals, the woman could appear six feet tall.

''Hey there, yourself.'' Sunny turned to Linc. ''I hear y'all brought home a little bit more than that prize-winning stallion you went after.''

''Yeah.'' Linc made an effort not to grind his back teeth. ''Two sway-back geldings no one wanted to bid on—both Appaloosas—and the buckskin mare Jack called you about.'' He passed Sunny the veterinarian reports he'd received on each of the horses. ''I want to unload the mare first so you can have a look at her.''

Feeling somewhat out of the loop, Tracy Lynn stood back while Linc, Jack and Sunny discussed the horses. She couldn't bring herself to move closer. She'd seen nervous horses being unloaded from trailers before, and the process didn't always go smoothly. The image of getting sandwiched between the barn wall and a high-strung horse's hindquarters still made her insides tremble.

Several of Linc's employees came out to lend a hand, including Hardy Pederson, who waved at her. Everyone stood clear, though, as Linc backed the first horse out of the trailer.

''Oh, my gosh,'' she whispered. Miss Helen was the color of the fringed buckskin jacket Tracy Lynn had bought on a whim and only worn once. Her head hung low, as if she didn't have the strength to hold it up. Judging by the ribs sticking out of her sides, it was a wonder the mare had the energy to even stay on her feet. The poor thing had been starved half to death.

Apparently Miss Helen decided that exiting her transport was as much exertion as she was willing to expend, because once she stopped, no amount of coaxing on Linc's part would get her to budge. Obviously mindful of her condition, he didn't attempt to use force. Sunny stepped in to assist, but she wasn't having any luck, either.

Just watching their efforts caused Tracy Lynn's stomach muscles to tense. She was practically leaning forward in anticipation, mentally taking the forward step for the horse. "Come on, girl."

As though the mare heard her barely audible words, it swung its head in her direction. Droopy ears, looking more like they belonged on a tired donkey, twitched, then drooped again.

Linc looked over at Tracy Lynn, and so did Sunny. Jack had already gone around to the other side of the trailer.

Why was she suddenly the center of attention? They were staring at her as though she'd been lip-syncing with a pretend microphone in front of a mirror. Or else... She quickly checked behind her to make sure nothing critterlike was sneaking up on her. Other than two dragonflies riding piggyback, the coast was clear.

When she turned back around, Linc and Sunny were still watching her. Linc motioned for her to come join them.

Her palms began to sweat, but she didn't hesitate.

Miss Helen tracked her movements until Tracy Lynn stopped next to Linc. "What's wrong with her?" she asked.

"It's hard to tell. It seems as though her spirit's broken. She used to be a runner, and from what I could find out about her, she's been stabled for a long time."

''Looks to me like she's been kept in solitary confinement and denied food. Why in the world would someone treat an animal this way?''

''Who knows? Why do some parents mistreat their kids?'' His gray-blue eyes turned flinty, but neither his touch on the horse nor his tone betrayed the inner emotion. ''Listen, babe. I know you're not wholly comfortable around horses, but for some reason, this one seems to be responding to you.''

''Because she looked at me?'' Tracy Lynn stepped a bit closer and tentatively stroked the horse's neck. It was fairly easy to act brave as long as Linc was standing next to her. She noticed that Sunny was very carefully checking Miss Helen's skin.

''I thought maybe it was your yellow sweater,'' he said. ''Horses tend to be drawn to that color. But for a second, her ear cocked toward you, too. And that's more response than I've seen out of her so far. Would you try walking a little in front of us, see if she'll follow? I'd like to get Miss Helen out of the way before I unload the stallion.''

''That stallion sounds like he's getting impatient,'' Sunny commented.

''I know. Do me a favor, Sun, and go tell Jack to keep everyone away from Matchmaker until I get over there. He's going to be a son of a gun after the ride here. The previous owner said he's not a good traveler.'' Just as Sunny left, a loud bang rent the air.

Tracy Lynn jumped. ''What was that?''

''Matchmaker trying to kick his way out of Jack's trailer.'' He adjusted his hat when a slight gust of chilly wind swirled around them. ''He's an expensive piece of horseflesh. He better settle down or he's going to hurt himself.''

The sound of hooves striking metal grew louder. Tracy Lynn could tell Linc was agitated.

She made a snap decision and reached out to take the halter rope from his hand.

''Go see about your stallion. I'll make an attempt to encourage Miss Helen to accompany me. We'll keep out of your way.'' Brave words, she thought. Hopefully, Miss Helen would recognize that she was a novice and take pity on her.

''Babe—'' The stallion banged against the trailer with more fury.

''Go, Linc.''

''Okay. But if she acts up or tries to bolt, just let her go. You hear?''

''Yes, sir.''

When Linc rushed around the trailer, Tracy Lynn glanced cautiously at Miss Helen. She hummed a little sound of distress because she'd never been left alone holding a rope with a horse attached to the other end.

''Okay, girl. I know my hands are shaking like mad. Try not to pay any attention. All we have to do is follow orders and we'll be fine.'' Acting as though she knew exactly what she was doing, Tracy Lynn took several steps, but was brought up short when Miss Helen didn't budge.

The sound of banging hooves coming from the other trailer were now joined by terse shouts of caution from Linc and Jack. Tracy Lynn retraced her steps, her heart thudding, her stomach sitting clear up under her breastbone.

"Don't be common, Miss Helen," she admonished, her voice sounding winded. "When out in public, one must always act like a lady. Stubbornness is not an attractive trait. Neither is embarrassment when you run like a scared rabbit—which I will definitely do if that beast over there starts backing in our direction. *Please,*" she begged, and was surprised when Miss Helen actually started without her.

"Oh. Here we go. See? This isn't so bad, is it?" She was quite proud of herself even though she was scared spitless and felt very close to throwing up. Helen's body kept bumping her shoulder. Worried about the safety of her toes, she tried moving away a bit, but Helen simply drifted with her.

"All right, you can cuddle. But don't step on my feet, okay?" She walked the horse well past the front of Linc's truck, not sure how to put on the brakes now that they had such good forward momentum.

"Um, we probably shouldn't go too far. Don't you think we ought to stop? Okay, fine. We'll go a little farther, but then we really have to turn around and head back. Otherwise, we'll end up in town, and I'm sorry to say, Anna can't allow you to come into the restaurant. That would be a violation of the health code. And I do wish you wouldn't hang your head like that. You're breaking my heart."

Helen followed her in a semicircle until they were headed back the way they'd come. "It sounds like things have settled down. I don't hear that stallion pitching a fit, do you? Good thing you didn't have to ride in the same trailer with him. Talk about acting common. He's certainly showing his tail.''

Experimentally, Tracy Lynn tugged gently on the rope, trying to keep her hand well away from the horse's mouth. ''Whoa. Oh, look, it worked. Aren't you a good girl?''

She looked up in time to see Sunny come around the back of the horse trailer and run smack into Linc's back. How long had he been standing there watching her?

''That was quick,'' she said. ''Did you really go see about the stallion, or were you just teasing me?''

''Turned out Jack had everything under control.''

''Hmm.'' She noticed that Sunny and Linc wore similarly bemused smiles. ''I see I need to give the two of you advice about manners, as well. It's not polite to eavesdrop—especially on a woman and a horse who are both shaking.''

Linc came toward her, relieving her of the lead rope. ''You never know what you might learn listening in on conversations a person's having with a horse.'' His smile became a teasing grin.

''You keep poking fun, cowboy, and I'll have the painters redo the walls in pink.''

''You wouldn't do that.''

''Of course I would. I love pink. I'm a girly-girl, remember?''

''Yeah, well, you're a cute girly-girl who's about to graduate to cowgirl. Thanks for taking over for me, babe. You've got grit beneath those fancy clothes."

"What fancy clothes? I'm wearing blue jeans and a sweater. Same as Sunny."

Sunny laughed. "Tracy Lynn, you couldn't look the same as me if you tried." She frowned. "Or maybe I should have said that the other way around. Your fingernails are manicured, your makeup's flawless, and your sweater is cashmere."

"So?"

"So, even your skin looks elegant."

"Say 'thank you,' babe," Linc coached.

Tracy Lynn fluttered her eyelashes at Sunny. "Thank you, babe."

"Smart aleck." Sunny motioned in Tracy Lynn's direction. "Linc?"

"I see it." As he spoke, he flicked something off her shoulder.

"What?" Tracy Lynn froze. "What's on me?"

"Horsefly. It's gone now."

She tried hard not to shiver but lost the battle.

"At least it wasn't a killer spider," Sunny teased.

"Of course not. We're much more civilized on this half of the ranch. *We* sweep away spiderwebs that lie in wait to attack our company." With her finger, she lightly touched the tip of Miss Helen's ear, jerking back when it twitched.

"Oh, sweetie. I'm sorry," she said to the horse. "Did I tickle you?"

Bending down to run her hands over Miss Helen's

legs, Sunny snorted. "Just because you like to have your ears rubbed, doesn't mean everyone does."

"You like to have your ears fondled?" Linc asked.

"Mmm," she murmured. "I love it."

"I'll have to remember that."

She met his gaze, held it. "You do that."

Sunny cleared her throat, but they ignored her.

Tracy Lynn could tell he was flustered by her comeback and decided to give him a break. "Why are Miss Helen's ears drooping like this?"

He dragged his gaze away and focused on the horse. "It usually means the horse has lost interest in the world around her."

"What can we do to help her?"

"You seem to be perking her up with your charm-school lectures."

"Okay, fine. Go ahead and make fun of me."

"Babe. I'm not poking fun. Well, not much, anyway. I'm impressed as hell that you've gotten this mare to respond—despite your fear."

The compliment thrilled her. She was pretty darn proud of herself, too. "Never underestimate a lady."

AFTER SUPPER, TRACY LYNN loaded her coat pockets with carrots and went out to the horse barn. The lights were on and the building was warm inside, but the wide center aisle was deserted. She'd thought Linc would be out here, and she nearly changed her mind and went back to the house.

This wasn't exactly her domain and she would have felt a lot better with someone at her side.

Grabbing her courage with both hands, she set off in search of Miss Helen's stall. The smell of clean, fresh hay permeated the night air. A few of the horses hung their heads over chest-high doors and she smiled at them as she passed, feeling stupid after she did so, and feeling guilty that she was playing favorites with Miss Helen. Until she received a formal introduction to these other animals, though, learned their dispositions, she'd stick with the one she knew.

"Hey, there, Miss Helen," she said softly when she located the correct stall. "I brought you a treat." The mare's ears lifted ever so slightly and turned toward her.

"How do you like your new room? It's nice and big, isn't it? Plenty of space to wander a bit and stretch out. And you have your own door and private backyard so you can graze. That's pretty cool, don't you think? I understand that the gardeners keep the grass nice and healthy. I'm sure you discovered that already since you don't typically see green grass in December."

She held the carrot between her thumb and forefinger like a pointing stick. Her hands shook, and so did the carrot, which annoyed her to no end. The horse moved closer, then snorted.

"Oh!" She jerked back and so did Miss Helen. "I'm so sorry. I didn't mean to scare you." Her voice shook, and she barely had enough air in her lungs to form the words.

"I'm such a ninny, but you probably already know that, don't you? I'm sure you can feel my fear. I really am trying to conquer it, so you'll have to be patient with me. Oh, what am I saying? You poor thing, you should be pampered after all you've been through, not worrying about my silly phobias." She spoke softly, keeping up the running conversation as much for herself as for the horse. With each word, she felt calmer.

"You see, when I was a little girl, one of my daddy's horses tried to turn me into a pancake. I realize now that it wasn't deliberate. Something scared it, and I was in the way. Not that I'm making excuses for myself, I just wanted you to know it's not your fault. How about if I set the carrot right here on the top of the door and you can come get it by yourself?"

From the doorway of the tack room, Linc listened to Tracy Lynn talk to the horse. He didn't know how Miss Helen felt, but *he* was thoroughly enamored.

He knocked softly on the doorjamb, wanting to let her know he was here without startling her. Her blond hair swished across her shoulders as she looked around.

"Miss Helen would probably appreciate daintier bites if you want to feed her a treat." He moved up next to her, took the carrot and broke it into several pieces, then placed one section in her palm. "Hold out your hand and see if she'll come to you. She'll nip the carrot with her lips, not her teeth. Her mouth will feel really soft, and it'll tickle."

"I hate it that I'm nervous."

"You're doing fine, babe. She likes it when you talk to her."

"How do you know?"

"Watch her ears. They're pricking up now, instead of drooping. And see how the insides turn toward us when we talk? She's curious, making sure we can be trusted. Here, turn your body slightly sideways." He put his hands on her shoulders and showed her what he meant. "This way you don't appear threatening."

After a moment, Miss Helen shuffled forward again and lifted her head enough to daintily nip the treat out of her hand. Tracy Lynn giggled. Her hand still trembled, but this time she didn't jerk back.

"See?" He had to smile at her excitement. She didn't let anything stop her, not even her fear. If Tracy Lynn set her mind to something, she went after it, no matter the obstacles, much the same as when she'd decided to get pregnant—on her own, without a husband.

In a small town, especially since she was the daughter of the most prominent man in the county, that had taken guts.

She fed another piece of carrot to the mare, then sighed. "I feel as though I've helped add two pounds to Miss Helen's skinny frame." Standing beside him, she leaned against him and rested her head on his shoulder, then reached for his right hand, the one that had delivered the punch. "How's it feeling?"

"I'll get to keep it."

She gave a soft laugh. ''Here we were worried about *me* starting a brawl.''

''I'm not proud of what I did, Tracy Lynn. After that bar fight years ago that landed me in jail, I swore I'd get a grip on myself, that I wouldn't be another link in the chain of violence and anger my father subjected my family to.''

''Oh, Linc.'' She stroked a hand over his back, soothing. ''That's not the same. You were protecting Miss Helen from a bully, not picking on someone out of meanness. I hope you turned the jerk over to the authorities.''

''Mmm-hmm. I took care of it. He won't be owning any animals for a good long while.''

She stood on tiptoe and pressed a gentle kiss to the corner of his mouth. ''Will you tell me how you got those scars on your back?''

He tensed at the abrupt subject change, and she slipped her arms beneath his unbuttoned flannel shirt, hugged him, then kissed the base of his neck just above his T-shirt.

''I know I'm prying,'' she said, her hands running softly up and down his back where shallow ridges bisected his skin. ''But you've got to let off some of your emotional steam. Every once in a while, you remind me of an old pressure cooker Suelinda used to have. It didn't have the escape valve that the newer models are equipped with, and it built up so much pressure the top blew off and splattered boiled potatoes all over the kitchen. We had to throw the whole thing away.''

''Nice image. Sometimes things are better off thrown away.''

''Not people. And you don't believe that for a minute. Otherwise, you'd never bring home these unwanted animals.''

He rested his chin on top of her head and allowed himself the pleasure of just holding her. ''My father beat me bloody with a horsewhip for crying in public the day of my mother's funeral.''

She gasped and tightened her arms around him. Since he wasn't looking her in the face, it made the telling easier.

''Then he picked up a broken fence slat and swung it like a baseball bat. That was around the time Jack came looking for me—I'd made the mistake of going with my father out to the old shed-row stable. Alone. By the time Jack found us, my dad had beat my clothes right into my body.''

Tracy Lynn felt sick.

''We might have had to bury our father that day, as well, if I hadn't pulled Jack off him.''

''Why didn't someone go to the sheriff? They would have locked your father up for child abuse.''

''I was sixteen.''

''Darn it, that's still a child!''

He shrugged. ''That just wasn't our way. We kept family business to ourselves.''

''Why wasn't your dad charged with drunk driving when your mother was killed? Or at least manslaughter?''

''There wasn't enough proof for an arrest. Maybe

the wreck sobered him up. Maybe the alcohol was out of his system before he called for help. The accident happened around ten o'clock at night. He didn't come staggering into the house until midmorning the next day. That's when he called the authorities. They found the truck wrapped around a tree. It wasn't visible from the highway. He claimed he was dodging a deer, that he'd been unconscious all night. The sheriff probably felt sorry for him because his wife was dead."

"You don't believe his story?"

"No. I think he sat in that car all night and watched my mom die while he waited for his blood-alcohol level to drop."

Tracy Lynn gasped. "Oh, Linc. Surely not."

"Babe. Everyone in town knew he was a drunk. But that night he claimed that all he'd been drinking was water—enough to flush out his system, is my guess. My dad hated water, said only sissies and women drank it. Mom always kept a case in the truck, though, for herself."

"That beating is why you never take the shortcut to the highway from Jack and Sunny's house, isn't it? You'd have to pass the old shed-row stable."

He looked away. "Pretty stupid for a grown man to hold a grudge against a broken-down building, huh?"

"Linc, don't. I can't begin to imagine being in your shoes. What's so remarkable is the kind of man you've turned out to be. Good and decent. You're not your father, Linc."

"Losing my temper like I did today makes me wonder. I've got his genes. So don't be putting me on a pedestal."

"Why didn't Jack tear down that stable when he built the new one?"

"I asked him not to. I wanted to see if I could reconcile my feelings about the past, go out to that old stable without breaking into a sweat and puking my guts out. So far, I haven't found the incentive to put myself on the line like that. It's like your memories of the horse that broke your collarbone. By steering clear of horses, you could put the incident out of your mind."

"But I'm confronting my fears."

"That's why Southern women are called steel magnolias. You're a lot stronger than us men."

She was a little surprised he recognized that. "So why did you come back and build this elaborate ranch?"

"It's an investment, babe. Business. And like I said, it's sort of a proving ground, you might say. Me against my old man, bastard that he was. The last time I was in that stable, I nearly died. Just thinking about it creates a rage inside me. Instead of growing dimmer with time, the memories just keep getting stronger."

She knew she shouldn't feel hurt by his statement, but she did. There was nothing in this world that could stop his wrestling match of painful memories. No one could rescue him from his demons.

Not even her.

Miss Helen moved closer to the stall door, and Tracy Lynn held out another piece of carrot. She suspected this sweet buckskin had bad memories, too. She carefully put her hands on the horse's cheeks, gently massaging in small circles, working her way to the drooping ears. They were so soft.

She decided to change the subject. He'd never promised to stay. That was just *her* wish.

"Sunny said you weren't sure if Miss Helen would live." She lifted the mare's ears, standing them up the way they were supposed to, then let go, disheartened when they flopped back down. "Do you really believe that?"

"I did when I bought her. Now that I've seen the way she acts with you, I think you just might be the one to bring her around."

"Really?" She grinned.

"Babe, I'm getting jealous just watching you massage that mare's ears and head. Who wouldn't respond to that treatment?"

Her eyes widened and she felt as though a powerful overhead light had just switched on. "That's it!"

"What?"

"Massage. It improves health and muscle tone, and it relieves stress and depression. Do you ever massage your horses?"

"Can't say as I have. I spend a lot of time grooming, though. Touch gains trust and forms a bond between a horse and his handler."

"Then you should teach the guys who work for

you how to give a good massage. Linc, you've got the perfect setup here. Oh, my gosh. This is such a great idea.'' She could feel her insides bubbling with excitement.

''Exactly what idea are we talking about?''

''I think you ought to open a spa for horses. Mainly cater to the elderly and stressed-out ones.''

He gaped at her as though she'd lost her mind.

She laughed. ''It's a fabulous concept, and I haven't heard of anyone else around who does this. It could tie in with your breeding business, too. Soothe the mares so they're in a better mood to get pregnant.''

''Soothe...?'' He stopped, ran his palm over his face, covered his mouth and stared at her over the top of his hand.

''That's right. And your stallions, too. Although it would probably be best to wait until *afterward.* We wouldn't want to get them too relaxed and mess with their performance abilities.''

''You and your ever-present causes. If you don't have three going at once, you think you have to go out and create a new one.''

''Have you ever been to a resort spa?''

''No.''

''Well, I have, and let me tell you, it's heaven. Do you disagree that these horses would likely benefit from a little pampering?''

''No, but—''

''Good. Don't worry about a thing. I'll take care of all the arrangements. When you see how well we do, you can incorporate the extra perk with your advertising.'' She swished her hair behind her ears. ''I'll go call Becca and find out if she's got any books on the subject. And I'll check with Sunny, see how well versed she is in alternative medicine.'' Once again, she went up on tiptoe and kissed him. This time square on the mouth.

''And you'll have to introduce me to the rest of the horses—especially the senior citizens in the bunch.''

He caught her arms before she could dash off. ''Babe. If you're of a mind to get into the business of massage, I'll gladly sacrifice my body in the interest of training.''

''Really?'' Her blue eyes darkened and her hands slid up the front of his T-shirt, then rested on his chest.

Linc began to sweat.

''Your room or mine, cowboy?''

He closed his eyes, his body as hard as an oak. ''I seem to recall you saying you wouldn't deliberately entice me.''

''Shame on me. I fibbed. Guess I'll have to go hang my panties on Bertha.''

He felt his lips twitch. Man alive, he was flat-out crazy about this woman. ''I've heard about that Sweetheart ritual, and you're not stripping in front of Storm Carmichael's kitchen window.''

''Bertha's not in front of his window—well, not *right* in front. It's closer to the lake. And who told you about our ritual, anyway? It's supposed to be a sworn secret.''

''Between the four of you girls, maybe—''

''Five. Tori's part of our group.''

''Whatever. No one outside your circle took any such oath, and—*Tori* is part of your group? You let my niece hang underwear out in public on the branches of some tree?''

''So far she hasn't had to. And it would be her *mother* letting her, not me.''

''I think I'll have a talk with my sister-in-law. Or my brother.''

''Be prepared to fall off your horse. Our Sweetheart rules were established twenty years ago.''

''What about this baby?'' His hands had slid to her waist, and his thumbs nearly met in the center of her abdomen. ''Are you going to let her fly her panties for all and sundry to see?''

The feel of him stroking her tummy where the baby rested in her womb was somehow more intimate than if they'd been making love.

Tracy Lynn's heart stilled, then started up again at a dead run.

Now who was doing the enticing?

She took a breath. ''I imagine our kids—Donetta's, Sunny's, Becca's and mine—will start their own friendship circle. For all I know, they'll change it to bras on the courthouse flagpole. Or jock straps if they're boys.''

''Do you want more children? Besides this one?''

Her gaze clung to his for a long moment. ''Yes. I

want it all. A big family, love…a forever commitment.''

When his hands dropped from around her waist, she wanted to grab him by the shirtfront and shake him.

But he'd never promised her forever.

Chapter Twelve

Linc wasn't used to this feeling of amusement and joy that infused him night and day whenever Tracy Lynn was around. Even now, he was hard-pressed to keep the goofy smile off his face as he watched her.

For the past week, she'd been diligently applying her massage technique to his horses—the docile and elderly ones, at least. She'd assigned several of the men to the more spirited mounts, reading them passages out of the book Becca had ordered for her.

She was still a little intimidated by the size of the animals, but with book in hand she was making peace with her equine charges and attempting to create a spalike atmosphere in which to lull them back to health.

He wasn't all that sure about the soft Celtic music floating from a portable CD player, but she insisted the horses loved it.

Linc had to wonder if she was actually accomplishing the serenity she intended, because more than once he'd had to soothe a spooked horse when Tracy

Lynn swatted at a gnat or a horsefly, or squealed and ran from a bee.

He was so intrigued and enchanted, he could hardly keep his mind on anything but hauling her into the house and into his bed. He knew one thing for sure: this self-imposed celibacy was wearing mighty thin, especially since Tracy Lynn made it clear that she didn't share his thinking.

Since he'd read the equine massage book himself, he went over to give her a hand. Ideally someone should be holding the horse's lead rope while the other person performed the therapy. Miss Helen was so enamored of Tracy Lynn, though, he doubted she'd move an inch unless Tracy Lynn asked her to.

Even so, he was glad to see that she'd made use of the eye hook on the outside of the stall to tie the horse.

"Need some help?" he asked. Miss Helen swung her head around, her erect ears twitching, the inside one turned toward him. In only a week, she looked like an entirely different horse.

"Sure. You can spell me for a few minutes if you want." She flexed her fingers, then settled her hands at the small of her back. "I think Miss Helen's sweet on you, anyway."

"Looks like you're the one who could use a massage." Instead of treating Miss Helen, he gently kneaded Tracy Lynn's back.

"Mmm, that feels wonderful. It would be even better if I could strip and have a bed under me."

He nearly swallowed his tongue. "That can be arranged."

"Promises, promises."

He spun her around, had her flat up against his chest in less than a second.

"Whoa," she said, breathless. "That was my fault. If I'd known today was the day you'd act like you meant business, I wouldn't have teased. I'm afraid I couldn't do you justice."

"What's up, babe?"

"Daddy, for one."

"You went to see him this morning, didn't you?" He continued to rub her back.

"Yes. He's so caught up in other people's opinions, and it's starting to make me feel really bad. Mama insisted he wanted grandbabies, but I'm beginning to wonder if she knew him at all. Do you know what he said to me?" She didn't wait for Linc to reply.

"He said it's a good thing the baby's not showing yet, since we'll be so visible during Christmas and the New Year celebrations. He has it all worked out in his mind that we should announce the baby New Year's Eve—the same time he intends to formally declare his candidacy for state senator." She rested her head against his chest.

"Want me to have a talk with him?"

"About what?"

"About butting into your life."

She shook her head. "You're a sweetheart, but I prefer to fight my own battles. You know, that massage feels really good, but I've got to sit down.'' She moved away from him and dropped onto the bench outside of Miss Helen's stall.

''What's wrong?''

''I imagine I'm just using muscles that aren't used to being worked. It feels as if the top half of my body's going to fall off the bottom half. Even my tailbone aches like crazy.''

''I'm calling the doctor.''

''Linc, I'm seeing Lily tomorrow.''

''No. You're seeing her today.'' He took out his cell phone and ratcheted through the stored names. He'd entered Dr. O'Rourke's office number in his database several weeks ago. At the time, Tracy Lynn hadn't thought it was necessary, figuring that the chances of him ever having to call the number were slim.

After all, by the time the baby was due, they would no longer be married.

But it was useless to argue with Linc once he set his mind to something. Truthfully, she'd feel better getting her OB-GYN's reassurance. Changes were beginning to occur in her body, and over this past week she'd finally begun to truly feel pregnant.

She stood up to put Miss Helen back in her stall, but Linc stepped in front of her and drew her against his side. It felt good to lean against him. He made her feel safe. Protected.

''Yes,'' he said into the phone. ''Thank you. I appreciate your help. I'll have her there in half an hour.'' He disconnected. ''What are you doing, babe?''

''At the moment, nothing. I *was* going to put away Miss Helen.''

''I'll get one of the men to see to her. We need to hit the road.''

''Wait.'' She tugged away from him. ''Have Hardy take care of her. She seems to like him the best.'' She went over and kissed Miss Helen. ''Sorry, sweetie. The bossy man over there is sweeping me off to the doctor. Don't you worry, though. I'll be fine. And I'll come visit when I get back, okay? Meanwhile, I expect you to act like a lady for Hardy.'' She slipped a piece of carrot out of her pocket. ''Here's a treat in advance. And you be sure to eat all your lunch. Anorexia is *not* in fashion, no matter what you see in magazines and catalogs. And—''

''Babe.''

She smacked a kiss on Miss Helen's nose. ''I'm coming.''

TRACY LYNN DIDN'T THINK there was a woman alive who ever got used to lying on an examining table—stark naked except for an ill-fitting paper gown—with her feet hiked up in stirrups. She stared at the ceiling as Dr. O'Rourke did a pelvic examination, checking her uterus and the size of the baby.

''You say you've been massaging horses?''

''Yes. And it's amazing how they respond to touch. I'm starting to feel as though *I* need a day at a spa, though. I'm sure that's what's causing my back to hurt. Sometimes I have to stand on a stool to reach the taller horses, and it's an awkward position."

Lily smiled. "I have to say, I never pictured you as a horse person."

"Neither did I. But I'm really enjoying it. I can understand my back muscles being sore, Lily, but should my tailbone be hurting like this?"

"That's a common occurrence with pregnancy. I do think you might be overdoing things a bit, though." Lily stood, took off her gloves and pulled out the leg rest. "Okay. You can put your legs down now, but stay right there. I want to do a quick ultrasound."

Tracy Lynn scooted up on the table, the sanitary paper shifting and crackling beneath her. "What's wrong? Is something the matter with my baby?"

"Calm down, Tracy Lynn. It's standard procedure."

"Will you be able to tell whether I'm having a boy or a girl?"

"It's a little early for that. You're only in your first trimester. We usually can't determine the baby's sex until the second trimester." She headed for the door. "I'll be right back."

Tracy Lynn's insides were a mass of jitters five minutes later when Dr. O'Rourke returned, pushing a portable machine that looked like a small computer monitor attached to a keyboard.

''Let's see if we can get a look at this baby,'' Lily said. ''Sorry, this is going to be cold.''

Tracy Lynn jumped and laughed as Lily squirted cold goop on her stomach—which was just now starting to look bloated. Before pregnancy, she would have been horrified by the sight and done extra situps to flatten her lower abs. Now she was proud of the slight roundness.

The monitor was turned so Tracy Lynn couldn't see it. ''Well?'' she asked, trying to get a look.

Lily swiveled the screen and moved the gooey roller from side to side, stopping low on her abdomen.

''You're definitely pregnant,'' Lily said. ''There's your baby right there.'' She pointed to a tiny white blob on the monitor, which was little more than a grainy image.

''But this baby's not a product of the medical procedure we did. You're only about three or four weeks into gestation.''

''But...'' Tracy Lynn's skin turned hot, her mind fuzzy. ''How can that be? I didn't have a period. The test came out positive. You said yourself that the urine test I did at home is the same one you use here.''

''False-positive results aren't unusual with the hormone injections we've been giving you. And urine tests aren't one hundred percent accurate. Am I right to assume that you and your husband have healthy marital relations? Or is there someone else involved?''

"No. I haven't—I mean, it's just Linc." Lord, what a mess!

She couldn't believe the errors that were compounding. The home-pregnancy test had been wrong. She'd been so excited, she'd jumped the gun and rushed off to tell her father—he'd ended up in the hospital, and she'd ended up married!

Then, having every intention of correcting a lie, she'd instead made it a reality.

And here she was, pregnant with Lincoln Slade's baby.

"Isn't it ironic?" Lily said with a smile. "We tried so hard using science, and all it took was the right man. Sometimes when a woman is totally focused on the outcome of conception, her body blocks the efforts. I suspect that since you believed you were already pregnant, you relaxed enough to let it happen naturally." Lily stopped and gave Tracy Lynn a shrewd look. "You *are* happy about this, aren't you? Having your husband's baby rather than an anonymous donor's?"

"Yes. It's just...unexpected." How in the world was she going to tell Linc? She calculated back to her wedding night. That put her one day shy of four weeks pregnant.

She should have been ecstatic. After all, countless times over the past few weeks, she'd wished that the baby she was carrying *was* Linc's.

Now she had her wish.

And the reality of that wish meant that she'd *really* trapped him now.

He wouldn't turn his back on his own child. He would stay with her.

She could have the family she'd always wanted.

But at what price? Linc's happiness? He had brutal scars on his body that went much deeper than skin. He was the strongest, toughest man she knew, yet he still couldn't face his demon.

He'd told her himself that he'd built his ranch as more of an investment than a permanent residence. He'd told her that here in Hope Valley, memories were triggered around every corner. At least at the Royal Flush—his ranch in Dallas—the constant reminders wouldn't dog his every move.

He'd worried that by allowing their relationship to become intimate, they might unintentionally hurt each other.

She didn't imagine he'd ever considered *this* scenario.

"Why don't you go ahead and get dressed now?" Lily suggested. "I'll stick my head out and let your husband know you're fine. He didn't look too happy about being asked to stay in the waiting room."

"Lily? Um, don't say anything about the changed due date, okay? I want to, um, surprise him."

The doctor smiled and winked. "Sure thing, hon."

Boy, what a surprise this was going to be.

LINC WAS SO RELIEVED when Dr. O'Rourke told him Tracy Lynn was fine. He knew how badly she wanted this child.

He hadn't realized until just today how badly he wanted it, too.

"Linc, this is ridiculous," Tracy Lynn said as he ushered her upstairs. "I can't go to bed in the middle of the day."

"Yes, you can."

"I'll just lie on the couch, then."

"You'll be more comfortable in my bed."

She perched her hands on her hips, lifted her brows in challenge. "Are you going to be in it with me?"

"Yes." He could see that his answer caught her off guard. True to her feisty nature, she rallied quick enough.

"Oh, for heaven's sake. You've got too much to do. *I've* got too much to do."

"That's the beauty of delegating, babe."

"But what about my horses?"

He grinned when she called them *her* horses, and she quickly amended her words.

"I mean, *your* horses."

"Babe. If we were in a custody battle, those horses would probably march right up to the judge and demand that he rule in your favor."

She laughed. "See? Now I've got you humanizing them."

"Yeah. I must be in bad need of rest, too." He propelled her to the bathroom doorway. "Get undressed. I'll go find your pajamas."

"Linc, I've only got a few sore muscles."

"And that's a few too many. I'll be right back."

Tracy Lynn decided she wasn't going to win this argument. She pulled off her boots, then her jeans and sweater. For all the undressing she was doing today, she should have just stayed in her pajamas in the first place.

Daddy and Ellie might have raised an eyebrow at that. Daddy especially. And she didn't imagine her lavender pig slippers would fare too well out in the barn.

The bathroom door opened a crack and Linc's arm appeared with her pajamas dangling from his fingers. She snatched them from him. When the door closed, she took off her bra and panties, then pulled on the soft drawstring pants and top.

Linc was waiting for her at the side of the bed. He'd taken off his boots and flannel shirt, leaving him wearing just his T-shirt and jeans.

"You really are getting in bed with me?"

"I figure that's the only way I'll get you to stay there. That mind of yours will start spinning, and next thing you'll be off supervising dominoes at the seniors' center."

"That's not until tomorrow."

"We'll get you a substitute." He pulled back the covers. "Hop in."

"I don't need a substitute. I'll be fine by tomorrow."

He propped pillows behind her shoulders and beneath her knees, then climbed into bed next to her and picked up his cell phone. "You might not be here tomorrow."

"I hope you know, I'll only let you get away with this bossiness for a very short while."

"It's called pampering, not bossing."

"Could have fooled me. Why might I not be here tomorrow?"

"If you're feeling up to it, I thought you might like to fly to Dallas with me."

"In your plane?"

He nodded. "Ever flown in a small plane?"

"No."

"Would you like to? I cleared it with Dr. O'Rourke. She said it would be fine."

She bit her bottom lip and smiled. "I'd love to. Why are we going to Dallas?"

"I sold a couple of my yearlings. The new owners are coming to the Royal Flush tomorrow to pick them up."

"You have baby horses there?"

"More like teenagers. And I've got quite a few pregnant mares due to foal next month."

"Really?" She shifted toward him. "My massage book mentioned that—"

"Forget it. You're not massaging my mares. The doc said you could fly, but you're still supposed to take it easy."

"I could at least talk to your men about the procedure."

"We'll see." He punched in numbers on his cell phone.

"Who are you calling?"

He chuckled. "You're supposed to be relaxing,

babe.'' He shifted the small receiver to his mouth. ''Sunny? I need a favor. Tracy Lynn's come down with a back ache, and the doc wants her to rest.... No, the baby's fine. But she's all worried about her horses not getting massaged back into health and friskiness.'' He glanced over at her and grinned. ''Yeah. She's in bed now. Suppose you can stop by tomorrow and see to things? I've got today handled, but I'm flying to Dallas tomorrow and taking Tracy Lynn with me.'' He paused and laughed. ''You got that right. I don't trust her. Okay. Thanks a lot.''

He held out the phone. ''Sunny wants to talk to you.''

''I'm fine, Sunny,'' she said into the receiver. ''Linc's just making a big deal.''

''You overdid, didn't you?''

''A little.''

''Linc just told me you're in bed, and judging by how quickly you came on the line, I'm assuming he's in there with you?''

''Sort of.''

''You can't talk, right?''

Tracy Lynn laughed. ''Depends on what the subject is.''

''You just want me to suffer,'' Sunny said.

''Of course. Misery loves company, don't you know?''

''Yes. Well, I want the full story when you get back from Dallas, you hear? And I want you to take it easy, too.''

''I will. You just see to Miss Helen. She's still not

comfortable around all of the men. Hardy does the best with her, but she trusts you more."

"I'll take care of her. Isn't tomorrow your day to go to the seniors' center?"

"Yes. I can call and let them know I'm switching days."

"No need. I'll take Simba over there on my lunch hour, and make Donetta come, too. You just take it easy."

"Thanks, Sunny. I feel silly that everyone's rearranging their schedules because I've got a few sore muscles."

"You'd do the same for any one of us," Sunny said. "I'll talk to you soon."

Tracy Lynn handed the phone back to Linc. "Sunny's going to drag Donetta with her to the seniors' center tomorrow, so that's one less thing you need to delegate."

"Good. Turn over and I'll rub your back."

Her heart thudded. She wasn't exactly in top form, and having Linc's hands on her was going to make her want more than just a back rub.

"Um, you don't have to do that."

"Babe. You give so much of yourself to everyone else. It's your turn now."

Instead of waiting for her to comply, he shifted her himself, tossing pillows aside.

"Relax," he said as he ran his palms over her tense muscles.

"Easy for you to say," she mumbled into the mattress.

''What was that?''

''Nothing.''

''I thought so.'' He chuckled. ''This is a clinical massage. Try to keep that in mind, okay?''

She had a lot in mind, but none of it was clinical. Every time his hands made a pass over her back, the slight pressure pinned her lower body against the bed just long enough to send a shot of desire zinging through her. Added to that was the baby in her womb. Linc's baby. He had no idea his hands were stroking so close to *his* child. *Their* child.

She wanted to tell him about their child, then wondered if maybe she should wait until Christmas Day—his birthday. Would he consider the news a wonderful gift? Or would it be a burden?

She couldn't think. The rhythmic stroking was turning her boneless and mindless. She couldn't remember the last time she'd spent the afternoon in bed. And she was feeling awfully sleepy.

LINC CONTINUED TO RUB her back long after her breathing had evened into sleep. It was hell lying in bed with her, touching her, knowing he wouldn't go any further.

He recalled her telling him that men either wanted her for a trophy or were intimidated by her. He was neither trophy-hunting nor intimidated.

He wanted her to know that her inner needs mattered. And that she damned well deserved to have someone take care of *her* for a change.

Chapter Thirteen

Linc banked the Cessna and buzzed Main Street in Hope Valley. From the sky at night, the town was breathtakingly beautiful. Christmas lights sparkled in candy colors of red, green, orange and blue, draped along eaves, rooftops and landscaping. The twenty-foot tree on the courthouse lawn was decorated with its traditional glowing candy canes, snowflakes and red bows with a three-foot-tall lighted angel resting atop its highest point.

Home, Tracy Lynn thought. That day in the hospital elevator, she'd halfheartedly suggested to Linc that she leave Hope Valley until the baby was born, but she'd merely been grabbing at straws. She couldn't envision living anywhere other than right here where she was born and raised.

Linc's roots weren't planted as deeply in this soil as hers were. Or maybe they were, but they'd been damaged.

As he lined up the small plane with the landing lights on the short runway at the Forked S, she couldn't help comparing this ranch to the one they were returning from in Dallas.

The Royal Flush was a beautiful, high-class operation but the home she'd toured had lacked the warmth and welcoming feel that this one in Hope Valley had. Maybe she was just prejudiced because she had a big piece of herself invested in this ranch.

The biggest difference she'd noticed, though, was in Linc's attitude. At The Royal Flush, he smiled and laughed with so much more spontaneity. He'd been at ease as he'd introduced her to Gus, shown her the pregnant mares, then strolled with her through the busy streets of downtown Dallas, helping her pick out Christmas gifts.

He'd been, in short, a happy man.

How could she ask him to trade serenity and happiness for bitter and painful memories?

Once they landed, he helped her out of the plane, and they unloaded their packages into the Suburban, which he'd left at the edge of the airstrip when they'd taken off this morning. The night air was cold, and she flipped up the collar of her coat as she climbed in.

Linc quickly started the engine. "The heater will warm you up in a minute."

"Should we check on the horses before we go to the house?"

"The men will have seen to them."

It didn't take long to get from the strip to the house. They decided to leave the packages in the truck until morning.

"I had a good time today," she said after he closed the front door behind them.

"Me, too. You were quiet tonight."

"Just relaxed." She didn't want to bring up her observation about how different he'd seemed away from Hope Valley. Having him care for her so tenderly last night, hold her in sleep, then being so close to him all day today had built a fever inside her she was tired of ignoring.

She was so afraid she was going to lose him, and that was tearing her up. January was when his mares would begin foaling.

When he would be going back to Dallas.

Granted, that wasn't across the continent, but it might as well be.

He walked with her up the stairs, and they both paused outside his bedroom door. She knew her heart was in her eyes.

"Come sleep with me," he said.

"Linc, if I come into your room, I'll want to do more than just sleep with you. I want to make love with you."

He cupped her face in his hands. "You are the most honest, straightforward woman I've ever known."

"You could return the favor."

"Yes. I can." He lowered his head and kissed her. She shivered and he rubbed his hands over her arms, then took her hand and led her into his room. "I'll start a fire."

"You already did that. A month ago."

He smiled, kissed her again. "I'm crazy about you, Tracy Lynn."

Her heart swelled with hope. Was that his way of saying he loved her?

She pulled her sweater over her head, her hair crackling with static electricity. While he stacked logs in the fireplace, she undressed and slid beneath the covers.

When he stood and walked toward her, firelight dancing at his back, her insides trembled. This fever she had for him was burning her up inside. He was a beautiful man. Broad shoulders, narrow waist and lean hips promised a sensual celebration for her hands.

His long hair was swept back from a face that could have belonged to a male print model. Women worldwide would flip through their magazines and pause, build unquenchable fantasies over those intense gray-blue eyes, imagine the skill of that unsmiling mouth, long to be the center of this man's universe.

Tonight, he was hers.

An odd sort of desperation mounted, a need so deep it frightened her.

She never once took her eyes off of him as he shed his clothes. And when he eased down beside her, his skin warming her from chest to toes, she wrapped her arms around him and held on tight.

"What's wrong, babe?"

She shook her head, buried her face in his neck

and kissed his heated skin. "I just feel...edgy. Like I want to pull you inside of me—all of you."

He rolled with her, shifting her beneath him, allowing her to feel every hard inch of him. Then he lowered his head and, with skill and tenderness, he toyed with her mouth. He took his time stringing soul-searing, individual kisses, each one sending her urgency higher, her love deeper.

"Linc, I need you so badly right now. It's been so long. I don't want to wait another minute."

He reached between them, his finger sliding into her warmth. She arched against his hand, sucked in a breath. He had to know she was ready for him.

"Come inside me now," she whispered. "Right now."

Holding his weight on his elbows, he framed her face in his hands and entered her. Slowly. Oh, so slowly.

Their gazes held, the connection and silent communication profound. Tonight was special. Different. She could tell he felt it, too.

He buried himself deep inside her, pressed, fusing their bodies so there was no telling where one ended and the other began. Making them one.

She'd never known stillness could create such an explosion of sensations.

"Linc—"

"Shh."

Her body pulsed around him, demanding more. But she didn't move, just let the exquisite pleasure grow. Stunned, her breathing heavy, she felt the orgasm building stronger, steadier, like a whisper in the distance, echoing back as a shout.

He swelled inside her, throbbing, so hot, filling her. So full. Her breath came faster, mingling with his. Chests heaved in unison. And gripping her hips, holding her absolutely still, he brought her to the most mind-numbing climax she'd ever experienced.

Powerful spasms shuddered through her, rippling from head to toe like a maze of dominoes set in motion, each tremor propelling the next one and the next as he, too, reached his own powerful climax.

And when he kissed her, the tenderness, the utter reverence felt so much like love it brought tears to her eyes.

THE FOLLOWING WEEK PASSED by in a whirlwind of Christmas preparations, laughter and a kind of contentment Linc had never known.

Tracy Lynn was in the house wrapping gifts, and he'd been banished to the barn. This is where he belonged, of course, but he'd much rather entice Tracy Lynn back into bed.

His cell phone rang, and Linc grinned when he saw the ranch's number on his caller ID. Christmas Eve was only three days away, and there was a dizzying array of things Tracy Lynn wanted to accomplish between now and then.

And because she was tied up inside the house, she kept thinking of things to remind him about that needed tending to *outside.* A person would think he didn't know a thing about caring for horses.

He punched the talk button on his cell phone and raised it to his ear. ''Yes, babe. Hardy remembered to give Miss Helen her treat.''

His words were met with silence. Heavy breathing. His smile faded and his muscles tensed.

''What's wrong?'' he demanded. ''Tracy Lynn?''

''I'm...the baby. I'm bleeding.''

He'd already started to run. ''Where are you?''

''The bedroom. Yours.''

''Don't move.''

Somehow he managed to push the right buttons to connect him to Dr. O'Rourke's office. He knew he must have sounded like a madman when the doctor herself came on the line after he barked at the nurse, who insisted on asking him questions to which he had no answers.

He raced into the house. He'd never been so scared in his life. He took one look at Tracy Lynn sitting on the floor of the master bathroom and scooped her into his arms as gently as he could. ''Hold on, babe. I've got you now.''

''I was looking for a heating pad,'' she said as though explaining her presence in his bedroom—even though she'd been sharing it with him for the past week.

He pressed a kiss to her temple. ''I called Lily,'' he said. ''She's expecting us.''

Although sun streamed in the windows, the lights were twinkling on the Christmas tree in the living room, and several more gaily wrapped gifts were arranged beneath.

She curled into him, her silence scaring him even more.

"I don't want to lose this baby."

"Shh. I know." The house smelled of cinnamon and sugar cookies. Scents of comfort, joy and expectation. He refused to believe tragedy could intrude on such bliss.

He carried her out through the garage door and eased her into the Suburban, figuring the ride would be a little smoother than the pickup. Leaning the seat back, he covered her with a blanket, stroked her forehead. "Hang in there, babe."

He backed out of the garage and slammed the SUV into gear. The town lay to the north, and the private, unpaved road heading toward Jack's house was the shortest way to the highway.

Every single rut the tires encountered felt like a giant crater, causing his gut to twist in another agonizing knot. It was a wonder he could even stay on the road, so focused was his attention on Tracy Lynn. He cringed each time a bump jostled her body, afraid the ride was causing her pain, doing more damage.

He was sorry he'd come this way, even to save precious minutes. Yet she never complained. Natural instinct made him want to slow down, but he kept his foot pressed hard on the accelerator, knowing they'd actually feel the jarring dips less at high speed.

After her backache last week, he should have made her stay in bed. Alone. He shouldn't have been making love to her. God Almighty. Had he hurt her?

She wanted this baby so badly. *He* wanted this baby. For Tracy Lynn, yes. But for himself, too.

He took the gravel turnoff, the Suburban fishtailing until the tires caught, speeding them past the shed-row stable and barbed-wire fences where Jack's cattle grazed in oblivious contentment.

Once they were on the highway, the ride smoothed out a little. The drive to town, though, seemed to take an eternity, and by the time he screeched to a halt in the ambulance bay at Hope Valley Medical Clinic, his nerves were so knotted he doubted they'd relax before next year.

"Stay put." He jumped out, sprinted around to the passenger side and carefully lifted her, blanket and all.

When the automatic doors opened, Lily O'Rourke was waiting. She studied him as though he were the patient, instead of Tracy Lynn. He wished to God he was.

"This way," she said. Turning, she quickly led him through the corridor and into a private examination room at the back of the emergency unit. "Lay her down on the bed."

His jaw ached where his back teeth were clenched. The nurses were all looking at him with a mix of apprehension and compassion.

"Linc?" Tracy Lynn said when he eased her onto the examining table.

He took her hand between his, kissed it. "I'm right here, babe."

"You're scaring the nurses."

Her brave, trembling smile made him want to cry. He probably *did* look like a warrior daring anyone to cross him. Icy terror filled him, and he imagined his eyes alone would chill a side of beef.

"No, I'm not. They're only pretending so I can save face. I think it's some kind of law that nobody's allowed to be scared alone in the hospital."

Lily began to fire orders that sent the nurses scurrying, then looked at Linc, a question in her eyes. "You'll need to let go of her hand," she said gently.

She wasn't asking him to leave. He wouldn't have, anyway. Releasing Tracy Lynn's hand was one of the hardest things he'd ever done. For some reason, he felt that if he let go, he'd lose her. His gut was tied in a knot that seemed to press against his throat.

He kissed her damp forehead, then moved behind the head of the bed, crossed the small space and leaned against the door that led to the back parking lot. He was out of Tracy Lynn's line of vision. This was a delicate situation for a woman, and he didn't want to distract her.

It tore him up to see her so vulnerable, and him being so helpless to do anything.

The nurses quickly removed her sweatpants and draped her legs for privacy. Linc felt dizzy when he saw the small towel—a towel that had come from his own bathroom. When he realized how it had ended up in the emergency room, he had to grab the wall for support.

She'd stuffed that towel in her underwear to stanch the blood.

Bright red.

Oh, God. That was too much blood for a woman her size to lose. His chest felt as though it was caving in, and right then, he began to pray.

Lily glanced at him, and he knew even before she gave an almost imperceptible shake of her head that something was very wrong.

That it was too late.

TRACY LYNN STARED at the water-stained ceiling, dry-eyed and alone. Dr. O'Rourke had tried to give her a sedative, but she'd refused. Why did she need drugs to calm her when she couldn't feel anything, anyway? Her hands were rock steady, her insides utterly empty.

She was numb. Devastated…and angry.

She wondered how it was even possible to be angry and numb at the same time. She felt the tension as if it were a separate thing, a part of her, yet not a part of her, a tight ball that coiled inside her, so huge she feared she would scream if she had the strength to care.

A remnant of a cobweb hung from the ceiling, swaying as the air circulated in the private examining room. Her mind skimmed over her life, the philanthropic causes that filled her days, the time and energy she spent catering to others…to her father.

She gave until she hardly had a spare moment, never turned her back on anyone else's need.

Yet the one time she'd taken a small detour, tried

to grab something just for herself, it had thrown everyone into a tizzy.

Well, now Daddy wouldn't have cause to be embarrassed, would he?

He wouldn't have to pretend his first grandchild was a preemie for the benefit of all the ugly-minded people who might be counting on their fingers the number of months from her wedding day to the birth of her child. The same people who accepted her offers to chauffeur them to appointments, donate to their causes, grieve with them at the funerals of their family members, lend her time and energy to resolve their problems or spearhead their projects.

What irony that her due date wouldn't have been an issue, after all.

If her baby had lived.

She twisted the band of diamonds on her finger. An unbroken circle of love. Typical of her eternal optimism, she'd allowed herself to get sucked into the dream.

A dream that was, in reality, nothing more than a sham. A nice gesture on the part of a man who couldn't accept emotional ties, but felt honor-bound to rescue. An expedient way to keep the peace, to calm the ruffled atmosphere so her father wouldn't have a stroke on top of his heart attack.

Now it was no longer necessary to pretend. She didn't need a white knight dashing in to rescue her.

She closed her eyes. All she'd ever wanted was to be loved without expectations—unconditionally.

And the one person who would have done just that, her child, was gone.

The door clicked open, then shut softly. Tracy Lynn didn't open her eyes right away. She recognized the sound of Linc's boots striking the tile floor. He'd called her father and Sunny. He might as well have shouted down Main Street with a megawatt bullhorn, because the clinic was now filled with well-meaning friends and family she didn't have the desire or energy to see. She just wanted to be alone.

Finally, she turned her head, opened her eyes. Linc's expression was grave.

"I feel so helpless," he said, lifting her hand and holding it in his. "I don't know what to say. Can I do anything for you? Get you anything?"

You can get my baby back, she wanted to say as she stared right through him. *You could say that you love me.*

"I'd give everything I own to make this better, babe."

At last, she focused on his eyes, feeling raw inside because she didn't have the strength to tell him the baby she'd lost was his. Once again, she realized, she was worrying about someone else's emotions.

For an instant, her numbness lifted and she wanted to lash out, hurt as she was hurting. But the urge couldn't overpower her love for him, the need to spare him pain. There was no sense in both of them being tormented.

"Money can't buy dreams, Linc." She hardly recognized her own voice, it was so hopelessly devoid of emotion. "God knows I tried to, with the two unsuccessful inseminations."

He started to reach for her, but she shook her head.

"I'm sorry," she whispered. "I just need to be alone for a while."

"Do you want me to send in Becca or Donetta or—"

"Not now. Tell them I'll call later."

He bent down and kissed her forehead. When he left the room, shutting the door behind him, Tracy Lynn got up. Her clothes were folded on a chair in the corner. The towel she'd stuffed in her underwear had kept the blood off her sweatpants, but her panties were history.

She dressed, then straightened the blankets on the bed. Removing her wedding band, she placed it on the mattress, then walked out the back door of the medical clinic.

She had no idea where she was going. She only knew that her body felt empty. She felt like a failure. And she couldn't even cry. The pain simply went too deep for tears. She couldn't make small talk with her closest friends, couldn't listen to another apology from her father, or another well-meaning suggestion that it was *okay* to let go of her emotions.

It wasn't okay. Nothing was okay.

The late-afternoon air carried the scent of pine from the Christmas trees crowded beneath an open tent across the street. She looked around the back parking lot, which was mostly dirt and practically deserted. Millicent Lloyd, her hair a slightly lighter shade of blue than usual, was just getting out of her 1965 Bonneville.

Several years ago, her father had approved funds to increase the main parking in front of the clinic, which was where most people parked nowadays. But Millicent babied her Bonneville, afraid the paint job would get a scratch.

Their eyes met across the expanse of broken asphalt, weeds and packed dirt. Without a word, Millicent walked around the car and opened the passenger door. In that instant, Tracy Lynn felt her nose sting, her throat ache. Millicent Lloyd was a shrewd, intuitive woman. It was as though she'd gauged the situation and simply known that Tracy Lynn was looking for an emotional escape but didn't have a clue how to find the right door.

They didn't know each other well, but right then Tracy Lynn realized that Millicent was the one person out of all the well-meaning friends and family who would understand at least part of the emotions she was feeling—or *not* feeling. Because not long ago, in one of those female bonding rituals that often took place at Donetta's Secret, Millicent had brought everyone in the salon to tears when she'd spoken so poignantly of the child she'd lost.

Tracy Lynn moved forward and got in the car. Millicent closed the door, then went around and slid into the driver's seat. The huge car engulfed the tiny woman, her head barely visible over the steering wheel. She didn't speak, just reached over and squeezed Tracy Lynn's arm, started the car and pulled out of the parking lot.

Tracy Lynn didn't pay any attention to where they were going. She didn't care. She closed her eyes and leaned her head against the headrest.

When she felt the car come to a stop, she opened her eyes and looked out the window.

They were in the cemetery. Parked at the curb a short distance from a familiar marble headstone.

Her mother's grave.

"Sometimes," Millicent said quietly, "a girl just needs to talk to her mama. You go on, now. Take your time."

And that was when the numbness lifted and the tears flooded. The ache burst into a tormented sob. "Oh, God. I miss her so much, Miz Lloyd. I want her back. And I want my baby back. Why did I have to lose them?"

AMONG A CHORUS OF PROTESTS, Linc managed to send everyone home. Trying to respect Tracy Lynn's wishes, he sat in the waiting room for half an hour, which was twenty-nine minutes more than he'd wanted to.

"The hell with it," he muttered, and strode back to her room. He pushed open the door and felt a moment of confusion. The blankets were spread neatly over the thin mattress, and for one hideous moment, he felt as though someone had died.

Someone had. A little life that had come to mean so much to him in so short a time. He walked up to the bed, his heart thudding, his palms sweating. When he saw Tracy Lynn's wedding band resting on the empty hospital bed, his eyes snapped to the chair in the corner. Her clothes were gone.

He felt a surreal sort of panic, his thoughts jumbling together, the terrible loss riding him like a dark specter.

He rushed over to the door leading to the back parking lot and checked outside, but the lot was empty. Next, he located the bathrooms, knocking, then poking his head inside.

"Linc? Can I help you with something?"

He whirled at the sound of Dr. O'Rourke's voice. "Did you release Tracy Lynn?"

"No. Why? Isn't she still in the examining room?"

"No." His hand tightened around the wedding band still fisted in his palm.

Lily's expression softened in compassion. "Women react differently to the loss of a baby, Linc. Sometimes they blame themselves, or feel ashamed that they can't cry, or think they need to go off somewhere and cry alone. It's not deliberate, or meant to diminish the father's emotional needs, but in the early hours or days after a miscarriage, a woman doesn't consider that her husband could possibly feel some of the emptiness she's experiencing." Lily put her hand on his arm. "I'm truly sorry for your loss, Linc."

Everything within him stilled. *You can't buy*

dreams. God knows, I tried to, with the two unsuccessful inseminations.

Two unsuccessful?

Realization hit him. ''She was carrying my baby, wasn't she.''

Lily looked stricken. ''Oh, Linc. I thought you knew. Last week—she said she wanted to tell you herself.''

But she wouldn't have. She had too much love and compassion, knew the battle he fought with his own demons. Didn't want him to feel forced to stay in Hope Valley as her husband.

Her strength humbled him. Tracy Lynn faced her fears, offered love without strings. She went after her dream, did whatever it took to hold on to that dream, yet tried not to sacrifice anyone else. She'd married so her longing for a child wouldn't harm her father's reputation.

Receiving the news that the baby hadn't been conceived at a doctor's office must have been a shock, yet she'd kept the news to herself. Not out of meanness. But out of love.

He turned back to Lily. ''How soon can Tracy Lynn safely try for another baby?''

''Three or four months would be my professional recommendation.''

Linc ground his back teeth.

''A couple of weeks would be okay with me, though,'' Lily continued with a sigh. ''I'll settle for whenever Tracy Lynn feels ready.''

He nodded, his throat too tight to speak.

A riot of emotions boiling in his chest, he strode out of the hospital, climbed into his Suburban and came close to dropping the transmission right there in the parking lot when he slammed it from reverse to drive before the tires came to a complete stop. He stomped the accelerator to the floor and never let up, not even when the speedometer needle pegged and he passed Storm Carmichael in his county sheriff's cruiser just outside the town limits.

Smart man, Storm went on about his law business and left him be.

Tires squealed on asphalt as the oversize vehicle leaned into the turnoff to the Forked S. No longer on the blacktop, the backend whipped like a sidewinder, spitting gravel in every direction. He cranked the wheel, bumped across the rutted grass and skidded to a stop in front of the shed-row stable. He was out of the SUV before it stopped rocking, an angry cloud of dust and pebbles blowing right past him.

"Come out of there, you bastard!" he yelled at the top of his lungs, striding forward. "You're nothing but a filthy rotten coward, and by God, I won't let you turn me into one, too!"

He ripped a board from the weathered fence, swung it at the post his old man had tied him to when he was nine. The support splintered and split in half. The roof extension shading the cracked concrete walkway gave an ominous creak, then sagged.

Driven by a blind fury, Linc pounded furiously at the structure, ignored the disintegrating shingles falling on his shoulders, the sweat dripping in his eyes.

When the fence board snapped in half, he flung it aside and used his hands, stripping off rotten plywood, kicking in the stall doors.

He wasn't sure when the rampage became therapy. With each decayed piece of material he pummeled, memories were purged, revelations uncovered, weights lifted, the ghost of his father driven out.

Breath heaving, he was brought up short by the sight of his brother leaning against the front of a crew cab truck.

"Need some help, little brother?" Holding a pickax and a claw-head hammer, Jack walked toward him. "You don't know how many times I've wanted to turn this place into a pile of rubble using my bare hands."

Linc wiped his face with his sleeve. "Thanks for letting me have first shot."

"You deserved it. You always got the worst of Dad's temper."

"Why?"

"I think because he couldn't break you. Other than at Mom's funeral, you never cried."

"Neither did you."

"Hell, yes, I did." Jack picked up a shingle and flung it into the field, giving them both a minute to pretend the admission hadn't been spoken aloud.

But it was that confession that gave Linc the opening to speak his mind. "I realized something when I was wrecking this stable. It wasn't so much the memories of Dad and the beatings that screwed with my mind over the years. I thought it was. But it was easier to hold on to the hate than to face that I was mostly just…embarrassed."

"Man, that dog won't hunt. I'm the one who picked shirt fibers out of your skin for three solid hours. I swear to God, I wanted to kill him that day."

"That's why I was embarrassed. You had the balls to stand up to him. No guy—man or boy—wants to admit he's not tough enough to fight his own battles, that he has to be rescued by his big brother. Don't get me wrong, I'm grateful. If it weren't for you, I'd probably be dead. Still, that doesn't stop the stupid voice inside me that makes me feel like a wuss for letting the bastard beat me."

"That's crap, Linc. Mom taught us to show respect, and raising a fist to a parent is one of the worst acts of disrespect I can think of. Even when you were a little kid, you had more honor and integrity than ten people put together. Dad exploited that. He knew you wouldn't hit him back, but just in case your integrity wore thin, he made damn sure you were too weak or injured to try."

Jack swung the claw-head hammer he held, smashing a hole in the side of the stable. "By damn, the word *wuss* shouldn't even be in your vocabulary." He dealt the building another blow. "And don't even ask me to prove that by arm wrestling or something." *Wham.* He clobbered the window casing. "I imagine you could shut me down in about two seconds…" *Wham.* "…and I'm not putting my ego on the line like that—even for you." *Wham. Wham.*

Linc decided against smiling, seeing as Jack had

two weapons in his hands. "You want to give me one of those demolition tools, or do you plan to hog all the fun?"

Jack looked around, his expression clearing. "Claw or the pickax?"

"The ax, of course. If you won't wrestle me, I can at least show you up by knocking down the biggest part of this eyesore." He accepted the tool but didn't use it right away.

The sky was a cloudless cerulean canopy that stretched over the abundance of their land. A good place to raise kids, Linc thought. A community that had heart and forgiveness. "Tracy Lynn lost the baby."

"Sunny told me. I'm sorry, Linc."

"It was my baby. The home-pregnancy test was wrong. She wasn't pregnant when we got married."

Jack swore.

"I think I might have lost her." He pulled the ring out of his pocket. "I've never seen her eyes so empty. She said she wanted to be alone, so I went out to the waiting room. When I came back, she was gone and this was on the bed." He opened his palm. "I'm not even sure where she went. Or what she used for transportation."

"Do you want her back?"

"More than I want to breathe."

"I know two people who can find her. My wife and my brother-in-law. It pays to have an in with the sheriff, you know." Jack set down his hammer and plucked his cell phone from the clip on his belt. "I'll call out the dogs, then let's you and me knock this worthless piece of history to the ground and bury it once and for all.''

''Sounds like a plan. But man, I sure hope you didn't just call your wife a dog. I'd be able to blackmail you for life.''

Chapter Fourteen

Tracy Lynn sat in front of the Christmas tree in Millicent Lloyd's living room, her hands wrapped around a mug of fresh coffee. Who would ever have thought she'd be slumber-partying with Miz Lloyd on Christmas Eve morning—her birthday.

Her trip to the cemetery and the day and a half spent with Millicent had been a time of healing for Tracy Lynn. The pain of her loss still pressed on her heart, but it was manageable.

She couldn't help but wonder if Linc had understood the significance of her leaving the wedding band, that it was simply her way of telling him he was off the hook, free to go back to Dallas if that's what he chose.

Life was too precious and too short to live with the wrong choices. She wouldn't wish that on him.

Millicent walked into the room wearing a navy-blue wool coatdress that made her blue hair look quite stunning.

"You look nice," Tracy Lynn said, glancing down at her own drugstore sweats.

After they'd returned from the cemetery that first night, Millicent had called Becca Sue and assigned her phone duty, so friends and family wouldn't worry over Tracy Lynn's whereabouts. Then she'd ordered toiletries, bikini panties and sweats from Chandler Drugstore and cackled over the stir such a request would cause.

Mr. Chandler had delivered the items himself, which had really tickled Miz Lloyd.

''Well, I figured one of us ought to appear presentable, since it's your birthday. You're liable to get caught in your pajamas if we have early callers.''

Tracy Lynn smiled, grateful she'd had this time to get to know Millicent Lloyd. The woman was a softie, always trying to hide her generous heart behind a gruff tone. ''Sit down and enjoy the Christmas tree with me. I'll run get you a cup of coffee.''

''You stay put, Tracy Lynn. I've already had my coffee limit for the whole day—although you made it so weak I practically had to help it out of the pot.'' Millicent sat in the olive-green upholstered recliner. ''You doing all right this morning?''

Tracy Lynn nodded. ''I'm okay. Thank you, Miz Lloyd. For taking me in and for knowing all the right things to say. You've been a blessing.''

''Oh, pshaw. I didn't do anything more than give you a ride—and set Darla Pam Kirkwell's tongue to waggin' over me wearing bikini underpants.''

''Do you think Mr. Chandler told Darla Pam?''

'''Course he told her. She was in the drugstore when I called. I could hear her trying out her imitation Marilyn Monroe voice on him. Last week she thought she was Mae West. She spoke to me on the street, and I was sure her girdle must be pinching." Millicent grinned. "Asked her about it, too."

Tracy Lynn laughed. "Miz Lloyd, you're something else."

"Yes, well, since we've talked about ladies' drawers and spent two nights under the same roof, you'd best just call me Millie. Besides, 'Miz Lloyd' sounds too stuffy. Especially for an old gal who's got half the town speculating about her underwear."

The doorbell rang and Millie sprang up. "Told you someone might come to call and catch you in your pajamas."

Before Tracy Lynn could decide whether to run or stay put, Millie had the door open.

She relaxed when Sunny, Donetta and Becca Sue came in, carrying gifts. "Hey, y'all."

"Hey, yourself," Donetta said. Setting down her package, she wrapped Tracy Lynn in a hug. Sunny and Becca Sue joined in, and for a long moment the four of them simply held one another, wordlessly.

When they broke apart, Millie was dabbing at her eyes and thrusting a tissue box in their direction. "You girls mop up before you drip all over my sofa."

"Yes, ma'am." Becca plucked a tissue and passed the box. "Might have known the rest of us would ruin our makeup, and Tracy Lynn hasn't even put hers on yet."

"Why is everyone so dressed up?" Tracy Lynn asked.

"Because we're celebrating your birthday." Donetta pointed to the gifts on the coffee table. "You already know we always get you clothes and make you try them on. We couldn't have you showing us up. Would you look at Sunny? She's wearing a dress."

"Well, I *am* honored," Tracy Lynn said. She wanted so badly to ask Sunny if Linc was spending Christmas with her and Jack, or if he'd already gone back to Dallas, but the timing just didn't seem right.

"I don't have anything against dresses," Sunny said. "I just don't see the need to wear them when half the time I've got my arm stuck up a cow's butt."

"A charming image," Becca said. "Speaking of uncouth manners, Miz Lloyd, did you know Darla Pam Kirkwell was over at Anna's last night telling everyone who would listen that you were flaunting your bikini underwear in front of Mr. Chandler?"

Millicent gave Tracy Lynn an I-told-you-so look. "At least I've still got the figure to look good in them. Darla Pam's got to pour herself into a big ol' girdle, poor thing. Now, like I told Tracy Lynn, I'd be pleased if you all would call me Millie. Especially if we're going to continue discussing underpants and cow's butts. I can't decide who's worse—you girls, or Birdie."

"Grandma Birdie," they all said in unison.

"Thank goodness for that. Tracy Lynn, are you

going to open these birthday gifts, or are we all just going to sit around with our teeth in our mouth?''

''I guess I'll open presents.''

When everyone was seated, Millicent handed her a box wrapped in lavender paper with a white bow. ''This one's from me.''

Tracy Lynn paused, touched. ''You didn't have to get me a present. What you've done for me these past two days has been the best kind of gift.''

''Oh, hush up and open the box. And if you don't like it, blame Donetta. She picked it out. Now, rip that paper. Nobody's going to use it again, and we don't have all day.''

Tracy Lynn laughed and did as she was told, then drew in a stunned breath. It was a long-sleeved, figure-skimming cashmere dress in the softest shade of poinsettia-pink. ''Oh, my gosh. It's beautiful! Thank you.''

Becca folded the dress as Tracy Lynn continued opening packages—thigh-high stockings and lacy blue underwear from Sunny, an antique pink zirconium barrette from Becca's shop, and a pair of strappy high-heeled sandals that were ridiculously inappropriate for cold weather and exactly the thing she would have picked out herself. Her friends knew her well.

''Come on,'' Donetta said. ''Let's go and watch you try on all your new things.'' They all piled into the large dressing-room area in Millicent's master bathroom to primp and fix their hair—a girls' bonding session just like the ones they had at Donetta's Secret.

The cashmere dress hugged Tracy Lynn's body, making her think of Linc and the way he loved to rub his hands over her soft sweaters. It had been only two days, but she missed him so much, she ached with it.

Determined not to spoil the party, she stood up to model the finished product—and nearly fell off her high heels when the very object of her thoughts strode right into Millicent's bathroom as though he had an engraved invitation. And it wasn't just his presence that stunned her, but what he was wearing—a perfectly tailored black tuxedo jacket.

The other women stood back. For a heart-stopping moment that seemed to draw out for eons, he froze, his intense gaze caressing her from her freshly washed hair to her brand-new sexy shoes.

"You take my breath away." They were the only words he said as he swept her off her feet and carried her out of Millicent's house.

"Linc? What in the world?"

Instead of heading for his truck, he turned and continued down the sidewalk.

"Honestly, Linc. Put me down." She checked to make sure her dress hadn't ridden up to the point of indecency.

"You're liable to break your neck in those shoes."

"These are cute shoes, and I can walk just fine in them. Where are you taking me?" He didn't answer.

They'd walked a block and a half, and the darn man wasn't even winded.

"I hope you know the curtains are fluttering in every house we pass. I'm sure the poor residents are afraid to even come out on their porches. Seeing an intimidating, unsmiling man in a black tuxedo—they'll probably call the sheriff."

No response.

"Might I remind you that people in polite society do not make scenes by carting women smack-dab through the middle of town?"

He turned and marched up the front walkway to the small white church they attended on Sundays, stopped at the bottom of the steps and kissed her.

And just that quickly, the outside world simply faded away.

She reveled in his strength, the solid feel of him, the way his kiss spoke to her. It was a kiss that inflamed, a kiss that touched her soul and made her want to weep.

A kiss that demanded she grasp onto hope and never let go.

When he lifted his head, his eyes were the color of steel. "I've never been part of polite society," he said roughly. "I was born to cause a scene, and I'll cart the woman I love through the middle of town if I damn well want to. Which I do."

For several moments, Tracy Lynn was rendered speechless. *The woman I love.*

From over his shoulder, she saw Millicent's Bonneville pull up to the curb. Sunny, Donetta and Becca were in the car with her.

Before she was able to find her voice, Linc carried her the rest of the way into the church. Her father was standing just inside the doorway. He, too, was dressed in a tux.

Her mind whirled.

Linc set her on her feet and tipped up her chin, his gaze holding hers.

''I love you, Tracy Lynn Slade. And I think you feel the same.'' He took her hand and placed it in the crook of her father's arm. ''If you do, meet me up there.'' He nodded his head toward the front of the church where Pastor Glen stood, then turned and walked up the aisle.

Tracy Lynn Slade. Her heart pounded and her body felt like a furnace inside the cashmere dress. She looked at her dad, then at her friends as they skirted her and preceded her up the aisle like bridesmaids.

The significance of the birthday gifts dawned on her. Something old—the hair clip; something new—the dress; something blue—the underwear; something borrowed…Donetta's shoes? They *did* wear the same size.

''That's a good man waiting for you up there,'' Jerald said. ''Gave me a piece of his mind. I thought he was going to take a poke at me, until I claimed age and illness for protection.''

''Is this your doing, Daddy? Because if it is…''

''I owe you an apology, honey. I was wrong to react the way I did when you told me about the baby.

Your mama used to soften my rough edges. Without her, I seem to have become a self-centered jackass. I hope you can forgive me. You could never be an embarrassment to me, and I'm sorry I took away your joy of sharing your baby.''

''There wasn't a baby, Daddy. Not then.''

''I know. Linc told me. You've been through a trial, sweet pea. I can't be one hundred percent sorry about my part in this drama. That man up there loves you. It's a parent's fondest wish that their child will someday find someone who sees all the wonderful qualities in them that the parent does, who will love and cherish their child as much as they do themselves. I see that in Lincoln. And I see the same thing in your eyes when you look at him. If you'll let me, I'd like to walk you down this church aisle and put your hand in your husband's. I won't be giving you away. I'll be officially, publicly gaining one hell of a son.''

''Will you still feel the same if we move to Dallas?''

''Can't imagine why you'd want to do a fool thing like that, but yes. I'll still feel the same. I'm through butting into your business—for the next week or so at least.''

Tracy Lynn smiled, her stomach jumping with butterflies. ''Then walk me down the aisle, Daddy.''

Linc's gaze settled on hers and never wavered as she approached on her father's arm.

The small church was filled with family and friends. Ellie, along with Anna, Storm and the grandmas sat in the first row on the left. Jack stood with Linc. Several wheelchairs lined the sides of the pews. Sunny, Donetta, and Becca stood opposite Linc, waiting for Tracy Lynn to fill the open space.

Oh, how she loved these people and this town!

But she loved her husband even more.

When he reached out and took her hand, she moved next to him, faced him, looked up into his handsome face.

''This feels a whole lot like a wedding,'' she said. ''Did you forget that you already married me?''

''I didn't forget. I'm a gambling man, and I took a chance I might be able to dazzle you with romance. I'd like to renew our vows, this time in a church and for keeps, if you'll have me.''

''I can be dazzled with romance.''

''Okay. Here're the stakes. I'm going to sell the ranch in Dallas and—''

''You are not!''

Murmurs and chuckles rose in the congregation. The pastor discreetly pushed the microphone forward, then crossed his arms, holding the Bible against his chest.

''You're happy in Dallas,'' she said more gently. ''When we were there, you smiled and laughed. Your joy was so evident. I can't let you give that up, Linc.''

''Babe,'' he said softly, reverently. ''Before you, I didn't have laughter in my life. You're what brings me joy.''

Oh, my gosh. Along with Tracy Lynn, every woman in the church sighed.

''What about the reminders here that trigger bad memories?'' she asked.

''Jack and I had a demolition party and buried them.''

''The stable?''

''Gone. Your courage in facing your fears helped me to face mine. Now I've got this huge, showy ranch on my hands that I can't bear to leave. A really smart woman told me the town needs a fancy spa for stressed-out horses. I think that woman would be perfect to spearhead the project. Acupressure, chiropractic, massage, the works. I'll even go for the music. Might add a little romance to the business of breeding.''

''I was kind of hoping that horses weren't the only thing you'd want to breed on that fancy ranch,'' she said softly, accepting the pang of grief instead of fighting it.

He took her face between his hands and kissed her gently, reverently. He rested his forehead against hers, his eyes liquid with emotion.

''I was going to tell you about the baby tonight,'' she said past the lump in her throat. ''After midnight when it was officially your birthday. I was hoping the news wouldn't bind you with unwanted strings, that it would be a special gift—for your birthday and for Christmas.''

''Ah, babe. I'm so tangled up in your strings I don't ever want to get loose. From the minute I staked my claim on the courthouse steps, that child was mine. Because it was part of you.'' His fingers lightly skimmed her hair.

''All I've ever wanted, for as long as I can remember, is you, Tracy Lynn. Every year you were my birthday *and* my Christmas wish.''

''You've got your wish. I never imagined I could love anyone as deeply as I love you.'' Her voice shook and she smiled. ''Now you'll have to think up a new birthday wish.''

''That's easy. I want babies with you.''

A huge sob echoed in the church. Grandma Birdie, sitting in the front pew, waved her handkerchief, indicating everyone should stop looking at her and carry on, then pressed the cloth back to her mouth.

''We'll work on that for next year,'' Tracy Lynn said. ''Meanwhile, tomorrow's your birthday. Do you have a more immediate wish?''

''Yes. A promise that you'll rescue this lonely rancher and let him love, honor and cherish you for the rest of our lives.''

''Absolutely. I will.''

Linc slid the wedding band back on her finger and kissed her until her toes curled. Then he looked at the pastor.

''Did you want to start the ceremony now?''

Pastor Glen gave a wide smile. ''You're doing a much finer job than I could ever do. I'm even taking notes, so please continue.''

The congregation laughed.

''Okay, if I'm going to show off, I might as well

do it right.'' He reached in his pocket and pulled out another ring, a diamond engagement band that he slid onto her finger with the wedding band.

''Good night, you weren't kidding,'' Tracy Lynn whispered. ''That's nearly as big as my eyeball.'' The gems in the ring held enough sparkle to catch the eye fifty yards away.

Linc chuckled. His society girl had just dropped every bit of her charm-school decorum. ''I am so in love with you. Where have you been all my life?''

She looked up at him. ''Right here waiting for you to come rescue me from old-maid status.''

''Good thing Becca Sue didn't hear that,'' Donetta whispered to Sunny.

Tracy Lynn glanced over her shoulder and smiled at Becca's frown. Because Becca *had* heard.

Turning back to her husband, she said softly, ''I love you, Lincoln Slade. And I promise to love, honor and cherish you for the rest of our lives. Are we at the kissing part yet?''

''Oh, yeah. We're definitely there.''